ROCK ME TO THE TOP

A GRACEFALL ROCK STAR ROMANCE

VICTORIA ZAK

Sign up for Victoria Zak's newsletter on her website to receive a free ebook copy of her Guardians of Scotland novella
Highland Destiny

You'll also find additional special offers, bonus content and info on new releases.

www.victoriazakromance.com
victoria@victoriazakromance.com

facebook.com/VictoriaZakAuthor

bookbub.com/authors/victoria-zak

instagram.com/victoriazakromance

twitter.com/VictoriaZak2

Rock Me to the Top: A Graceful Rock Star Romance
Victoria Zak
Copyright 2021 by Victoria Zak

Cover Design by JAB Designs

❀ Created with Vellum

This series is dedicated to the wild at heart. Rock on!

1

*T*he meeting room at Clef Tonic Records went silent. The breathtaking news surged through Joe, forming a lump in his throat that left him speechless. It was finally happening. Seven years of hustling the rock scene, gigging from city to city, and paying his dues had finally paid off. Gracefall had landed their first major headlining world tour.

This punk kid's dream was now becoming a reality. Joe scrubbed a hand down his face. *Headliners.* He glanced at his younger brother, Dylan, who was sitting across the table, his face beaming with enthusiasm. Little bro mouthed, "Holy shit, dude."

Joe's heart pounded in double time as Moxley, their guitar player, shot him the same stunned expression.

Big Rick, the president of Clef Tonic Records, was on the other end of the conference call going on about details of the tour, but Joe couldn't hear them over his thundering heartbeat. Excitement brewed. *Headliners.* The word looped inside his brain—a beautiful song he'd never get tired of hearing.

"Davidson," Rick barked through the cellphone placed in the middle of the office table. "Make sure you have your boys on the bus by the end of the week." He inhaled deeply, then exhaled as though he'd taken a long drag from his celebratory cigar. "We need to strike while the iron's hot."

Davidson, their band manager, cleared his throat as he, too, was experiencing the excitement pulsing in the air. "Yes, sir. That won't be a problem."

"Horns up, boys." Rick's raspy voice rang out loud and clear. "Welcome to the big time." The call ended, and the room came alive.

Moxley shot out of his chair like a cannon and made a beeline straight to Joe. They met in the middle in a firm hug. "We finally did it, bro." Mox pounded his fist against Joe's back, overjoyed.

On the outside, Joe played it cool, as usual. As the only two members of Gracefall with their heads screwed on halfway straight, he and Moxley kept themselves on lockdown around the rest of the crew. Most of the time they succeeded.

Good ole *Steady Joe,* the glue that had held Gracefall together throughout the years. That side of him was all the crew saw as he slapped Mox on the back. But on the inside, he was stoked!

Financially, this couldn't have happened at a better time. Moxley's wife was due with their first child. Tyler could finally afford his extravagant bass guitar collection without maxing out credit cards. And Dylan, now watery-eyed and shooting him a smile over Tyler's shoulder, would never have to return to their childhood home.

In two big strides, the brothers met with a shoulder bump. Overwhelmed with emotions, Joe pulled him into a tight hug.

Together they had formed a band, played gigs every night since high school, felt the grit of being on the road. Giving up had never been an option. Their dream was coming true.

"We did it." Dylan squeezed him harder.

Joe's chest tightened as tears stung his eyes. "Fuck."

Clearing his throat, he stepped back and nonchalantly wiped his face with the back of his hand. This was much more than just making it to the top. He had removed Dylan and himself from the trailer park, and from Karen, the demon bitch attached to a subhuman host who called herself their mother.

"It wouldn't hurt to smile, a-hole." Dylan shoved him playfully.

Joe glanced at his bandmates, who were waiting for his reaction. These guys were his family—he would do anything for them. They deserved this as much as he did. Maybe it was time to stop looking down and let himself enjoy the view at the top for once.

A smile spread across his lips, and it felt good, damn good. Excitement exploded inside him. He grabbed Dylan into another hug, lifting him off the ground. "Fuck yeah!"

The room came alive as Tyler and Moxley joined them in a group hug.

Joe motioned for Davidson to join them, and he did, adding another cheering layer.

So many emotions filled the room. Joe was on top of the world, and he wasn't looking back.

The celebration continued as they piled into the elevator, making their way to the parking garage. Moxley whipped out his cellphone. Joe knew exactly who he was calling.

"Hey, baby," Moxley smiled. "Guess what?"

The screams on the other end of the cell echoed through the elevator.

Joe was happy for him, and to be honest, a little jealous. He had almost everything Mox had, except the one thing that made all the difference—a beautiful wife to share the news with.

"We need to celebrate," Tyler said. "Beers at my place."

"And women," Dylan added.

"I'll make some calls." Tyler winked as he pulled his phone from his back pocket.

"No parties." Joe broke up the soiree before it had started. "We have to be on the bus in four days—not hungover."

Dylan put his arm around him. "Live a little, bro. We can sleep it off on the bus."

"That's if you make it to the bus." Their parties always started out as innocent drunken shenanigans that escalated to blitzed-out chaos, leaving Joe to pick up the pieces the next day and herd their hungover zombie asses to their next gig. Their shit got old.

"Joe's right." Moxley shoved his phone in his leather jacket pocket. "We can't mess this up."

Their first stop was at Dylan and Tyler's floor. "Don't worry, mother hen." Dylan backed out of the elevator as the doors opened. "We'll be there on time." The silver doors began to slide shut as little bro pounded his fists together, then gave Joe and Moxley double middle fingers.

"He's your brother, man," Mox shook his head.

Joe snickered. "Yep, no changing that."

The elevator stopped on the next floor. He and Mox got out and made their way to their cars. Being back home in California brought back some amazing memories, and some not so good ones. He may not have a wife, but there was someone special. Someone he wanted to share their amazing news with. But it was complicated.

"So how do you do it, man?" Joe shoved his hands in the front pockets of his Levi's. "How do you keep it all together?"

Mox leaned against his black Toyota Tacoma bumper and pulled a pack of Marlboro Reds from his jacket. He lit one up. The dude was old-school cool with his super stylish pompadour mullet hairstyle. Joe had never met anyone more easy-going and loyal than Mox.

"Phone sex." Mox took a long drag from his cigarette, then leaned back and exhaled.

"What?" Joe coughed incredulously.

"Yep." Mox repeated dryly, squinting as he took another drag. Then he winked at Joe. "FaceTime is a game changer."

Seriously? That's all it took? Hell yeah, he could get into that kind of kink, especially with Mel.

"I'm serious, though. How do you do it?"

"I'm not joking." His bandmate ran his hand through his jet-black hair. "Why do you think I don't hang out after the shows? I hightail it back on the bus to call my girl."

He gave his friend a raised brow. "Too much information."

Mox took another drag. "Listen, Joe, there's a lot of temptation out there, and it's only going to get worse. You have a good head on your shoulders. Find a woman who'll keep you grounded. It's the only way to keep your sanity in our crazy world."

"I'm not so sure it's fair to bring someone like that into our world." Joe sat down next to Mox on the rear bumper. His childhood best friend, Melody Sterling, had been on his mind ever since his plane had landed at LAX the night before.

At thirteen, he'd been the kid from the wrong side of

town. Eleven-year-old Mel had been rock and roll royalty, the only daughter of the God of Thunder, Leo Sterling. The second-best thing that had ever happened to him had been answering a small ad in *DrumBeat Magazine*:

Play to Perfection
High Energy
Cheaper than Ritalin
Leo Sterling's "Drum Like a Pro" Lessons

The only thing that topped that, the only thing that ever could, was having Mel for a best friend.

Moxley flicked his cigarette onto the ground, then stubbed it out with the bottom of his boot. "Call her."

He didn't have to mention Melody's name. Mox knew Joe had been thinking about her.

Their FaceTime calls had stopped. Their lives were busy. He'd been in New York promoting Gracefall's third album. She'd been absorbed in cello auditions for the Los Angeles Orchestra. He understood how important it was to her, but damn, he missed her. Especially her smile. He missed the phone calls where they'd stay up late talking and giving each other advice.

There was never a time when Mel wasn't in his life. So, two weeks without talking wasn't flying with him.

"You're right." He took his phone out. "I'll call her. She'll want to know the good news."

"Right," Moxley scoffed.

"What?" Joe walked over to the driver's side of his Jeep, pausing before getting in.

"As long as you tell her at a fancy restaurant over filet mignon," Mox said sarcastically as he opened the door to his truck and slid in.

Joe flashed Mox the peace sign as he climbed up into the driver's seat. He snickered—that wouldn't be awkward at all. He'd be crossing the friends-to-lovers line; a line Mel and he had protected throughout the years. They cherished their friendship and had never toyed with being more than friends.

But something had changed for him. There wasn't any other woman he could picture spending the rest of his life with. But with Melody, he could. She was home.

He punched in the security code, unlocking his phone. Taking in a deep breath, he brought up his favorites list, and first on the list was Melody Sterling. He tapped on the mobile icon and waited for it to ring.

His heart raced, which was ridiculous. He shouldn't be nervous. He'd called Mel thousands of times. Today was no different. At least, that's what he told himself.

"Hello." With the music thumping in the background, he didn't recognize the voice.

"Um, hey, this is Joe. Is Mel around?"

"Oh, thank God you called," the woman shouted over the noise, sounding distressed.

"Dani, is that you?" He struggled to make out her voice.

"Yeah. Are you in town?"

"Yeah."

The background noise muffled like she'd covered the phone. "Don't do it, Mel!"

Joe's heart nose-dived straight into his stomach. "Do what?" he exclaimed. "Is Mel in trouble? What's going on?"

"She's had a really shitty day. Three Mind Erasers later, and she's out of control. She's threatening to dance on the table."

"Fuck." He revved up the Jeep and slammed it in reverse.

"Where are you?" His tires squealed around every turn as he worked his way out of the parking garage.

"Dragon's Brew on the strip."

Sunset Strip was a good thirty minutes from where he was, not counting traffic. "I'm on my way."

"Hurry. She's lost her damn mind."

"Just keep her off the table, okay?"

"I'm not promising anything. I've never seen her like this. Please hurry."

The phone went silent as his Jeep shot out of the garage, barely missing a pedestrian. The stop-and-go traffic through the city drove him crazy. He couldn't get to the bar fast enough. Mel, drunk? This wasn't like her at all. He glanced at the clock on the dashboard. It was only six o'clock at night. Whatever it was couldn't be *that* bad.

2

*H*olding a wonderfully tall, and most importantly, *cold* glass of amber ale, Melody sashayed—

"Watch it!"

Okay, maybe sashaying was a little too complicated. "Sssorry," she apologized as she steadied herself, and the amber ale, and heel-toed it back to the table where Dani sat. "It's sooo hot in here." She held the cold glass to her cheek before taking another satisfying gulp. "Who called?"

"Joe." Dani crossed her arms, making it known she wasn't happy with her.

"Oh! My! God!" Melody slammed the glass down and grabbed her cell. "Joe!" she yelled into the phone.

"He already hung up." Dani rolled her eyes.

"Did he say he was in town?" She sat on the barstool across from Dani.

"He is."

A huge smile stretched across her lips. It had been so long since she'd seen him. "I should call him back." She squinted, trying to make out the numbers on her phone.

Everything was a blur. She should've stopped at the second Mind Eraser.

Dani took her cell. "You'll see him soon enough." She tipped her chin toward the glass. "Where did you get that?"

"I almost forgot." Melody snorted. "See those guys sitting at the bar?" She glanced over her shoulder, giving them a flirty wave.

"Stop that." Dani grabbed her arm. "You don't know those guys."

Shrugging, she picked up the beer to take another sip. Her friend was really killing her buzz.

"And don't drink that." Dani took the glass away, and beer sloshed over the brim. "They could have slipped something in it." She leaned back and set the glass down on the table behind her.

Melody inched forward and lowered her voice. "Like drugs?" she mocked, laughing.

"I'm serious. Guys that hang out in bars are always up to no good. Drunk women are easy prey."

Dani was amazingly gorgeous with long, dark hair, crystal-blue eyes, and olive skin. With those striking features, she'd never been lonely for very long. During Melody's freshmen year at UCLA, she'd met Dani, and they had been friends ever since. Dani was like the sister she never had.

They had a lot in common—they both had famous parents. Because of this, they understood the ups and downs of living in the limelight. Sometimes it wasn't a glowing experience, especially when the media had the tools to destroy a person's reputation. That year, Melody's family had been under attack by the media over a situation blown out of proportion. It had been reported that legendary drummer, Leo Sterling, had called the police on his estranged ex-wife. Apparently, she had shown up drunk at his estate and punched him in the face for writing a chapter in his tell-all rock star biography, *Leo Sterling: The God of Thunder*, which claimed she was the groupie that never left. It was all a misunderstanding. Dirty laundry was something normal families could handle without paparazzi, but since hers was in the limelight, it was all hung out for everyone to see.

The truth was that the chapter in her father's book wasn't about his ex-wife. Leo got a black eye that night, and the police were called by a maid who didn't understand the commotion going on. Her mother wasn't charged with assault. She was an alcoholic, so she went back to rehab. Through it all, Dani had been there, a true friend helping her put everything into perspective.

Melody held her friend's hand from across the table. "That's why you're here to keep me out of trouble."

"Mel, I have never seen you this drunk before. Taking a drink from a stranger?" She shook her head. "You have no street smarts."

And why would she? Being the daughter of a legendary rock and roll drummer, her school of hard knocks was in a different discipline altogether. Her family lived the rock star lifestyle, and it had torn her mother and father apart. Her mother lived the life of a musician's wife, and it was hard for her to compete with other women, whiskey, and rock and roll. Her father lived to perform his music—nothing would change that.

And Melody had kept her family together. On the straight and narrow. She was the responsible one. She worked hard, focused on her lifelong dream of becoming a cellist for the Los Angeles Orchestra. Her life had been centered around that dream, until tonight.

"If everything you've ever worked for was smashed into a

million pieces, you'd want just one night to feel bulletproof, wouldn't you?" Feeling her buzz wearing off, Melody grabbed her friend's beer and took a sip.

"I'm sorry you didn't make the cut," Dani consoled. "But get over it. There are other orchestras out there that would die to have you."

"Ouch, brutal much?" It was just like Dani to hit her with the hard truth. There was no coddling or feeling sorry for her. Dani gave her opinion, even without being asked, but that's what she loved about her friend. She was real.

"Playing with the LA Orchestra is my dream. I won't accept anything less. I blew it." The auditions had been vicious. There were three auditions, and she'd made it through all three, feeling confident until she received the dreaded call.

"Well, I'm blaming Drew." Dani sneered. "He should've waited until after the auditions to break up with you."

"Oh jeez, thanks for reminding me of another failure." Drew, her on-again, off-again boyfriend for the past year, broke up with her on the last day of her auditions. As much as she would like to use Drew as an excuse for her failure, he wasn't the reason. Plain and simple, she wasn't good enough.

Melody shrugged it off. She never really clicked with Drew. Their relationship was missing something, and she couldn't put her finger on it. He was handsome in a classic good boy, great in bed way. He treated her well, but he had a problem sharing her with her cello. He didn't understand; practice came first.

A wave of guilt reared its ugly head. Had she ignored him too many times? Could she have nurtured their relationship better? Took the time to really get to know him?

She waved down the waitress, motioning for two more rounds of shots. Whatever the reason, it was too late now.

Dani shook her head. "Girl, you're going to be hurting tomorrow."

"I don't care. I want to forget today even existed." She slapped her hands down on the table. "So, let's go make fools of ourselves. I won't remember a thing."

The waitress returned with the drinks. She threw back one shot. The amber liquid burned going down, but not for long. Finished, she slammed the shot glass down, feeling recharged again.

In a haze, she peered out over the bar looking for trouble. The Dragon's Brew was where people gathered to have a few drinks before the clubs opened. The place was old. The walls were covered in dark walnut wood panels. It smelled earthy—a mixture of stale cigarettes and whiskey. Red and black leather couches bordered the room. She and Dani sat among the fifty high-top tables in the middle. Every table was full.

"Are you ready?" A woman's voice came through the speakers.

Melody turned her attention to the bar at the back of the room, trying to see who was talking. She squinted against the bright inlay lights surrounding the liquor shelf behind the bartender. *Ready for what?*

"Hella Good" by No Doubt thumped through the speakers as the crowd made a mad dash to the bar.

"Who wants to dance?" the woman yelled as two gorgeous lady bartenders in low-waist jeans and tailored, cut Dragon's Brew t-shirts danced on top of the bar.

Wide-eyed, she shot Dani an excited smile.

"No!" Dani shook her head. "No way."

"Come on," Melody begged, "Live a little."

Overcome by the excitement in the room, Melody climbed off the barstool. She didn't care if Dani didn't join her—she was dancing.

"I'm doing it." She shouldered her way through the crowd to the back of the room. A big biker clad in head-to-toe leather stood next to the bar watching the girls on stage. She tapped him on the shoulder.

He turned around, liking what he saw.

"Give me a lift?" She motioned to the stage.

"Hell yeah, Darlin'." He wrapped his meaty hands around her waist and hoisted her up onto the bar with all the grace of a bull in a china shop, but *finally*! She was dancing! And it felt incredible! The crowd went wild.

～

*A*n hour later Joe pulled into the parking lot next to Dragon's Brew. A whole hour! He prayed he wasn't too late as his tires crunched over the gravel and he skidded to a stop in the first empty spot he saw.

The sun had gone down, and the Strip had come alive. A long line of people formed outside of The Whiskey, a club across the street, reminding him of the days Gracefall had played there. Things hadn't changed one bit.

Joe rounded the corner as two women walked past. They turned and did a double take. "Joe Grace? From Gracefall?" one of them asked from behind him.

He didn't look back and ducked inside before the women caught up. Everyone was crowded at the back of the bar. As he peered over the sea of people, he froze.

Mel was dancing on the bar.

MEL.

Dancing.

On the bar.

His Mel.

His always serious, always in control, always...*Mel* was....

He stood there for a moment, taking her in.

She lifted her arms above her head, and her black silk blouse rose, showing more skin than he wanted everyone to see. Her hips swayed, hypnotizing him as though she danced only for him.

Her long, dirty-blonde hair was pulled back into a messy braid that fell over her shoulder, stopping below her breast. Toned, California sun-kissed legs contrasted nicely against her white leather short shorts.

God, she was as beautiful as he remembered.

A burly man twice Joe's size (and he was no lightweight) pawed at her leg. Mel pushed the big man away with her foot playfully, which only added fuel to the dude's fire. He grabbed her again, this time clutching her thigh, making her recoil in obvious distress. Something primal came over Joe as he shoved his way to the front of the crowd.

He sized up the man, assessing his chances of taking him on. Given he wore a black leather vest with a skull logo on the back, the dude was probably a biker and most likely not alone. Joe was a big guy. He could take him. He was no stranger to bar fights. In the early stages of Gracefall's career, there were always hecklers at their shows. Moxley got to a point where ignoring the insults was no longer an option. He'd throw down his guitar and jump the idiots with flying fists. The next thing Joe knew, he was joining in on the fun. No one disrespected his friends or his band.

However, as he'd guessed, this dude had backup. A quick scan confirmed several big guys in the same black leather vests standing nearby. Best to grab Mel and get the hell out of dodge.

"Melody!" he yelled over the loud music.

She glanced down at him, and her face lit with the biggest smile. "Joe?"

He reached for her hand. "Come on down, baby."

She bent down. "What? I can't hear you."

He felt the biker dude's angry gaze on the back of his head. "Let the bitch dance. I'm enjoying it."

It took all of Joe's resolve not to turn around and punch the guy in the mouth. He had to get Mel off the bar and get out of there fast.

He motioned for her to come closer, and when she did, he pulled her onto his shoulder.

"What are you doing?" she laughed.

"Getting us the hell out of here." He made a beeline toward the door, praying the biker dude didn't follow.

"Put me down!" she wiggled against his grip. "I'm not done dancing!"

"No, I won't, and yes, you are!" He pushed through the crowd.

"Fine," she surrendered. "Guess I'll have to announce to everyone I'm being abducted by a rock star," she teased.

"You won't." He prayed she wouldn't. No one else had recognized him yet. But she was drunk. Shit was going down.

"Oh my god! It's Joe Grace from Gracefall," she shrieked like a crazed fan.

The noise in the bar was too loud. No one heard her.

He slapped his hand across her ass. "Stop it. I really don't feel like getting my ass kicked tonight."

"You're no fun." She smacked his ass, returning the favor.

"Joe! Mel!" Dani yelled behind him, but he kept moving toward the door.

The fresh night air was welcoming as he reached the parking lot. Lucky for him, he made it out without being noticed by fans.

"You can put me down now, neanderthal," Mel laughed. "We're outside."

Right. He set her down by his Jeep. "What were you thinking?" He shoved his hands through his hair. "You could've gotten hurt."

She eyed him for a moment as she leaned against the Wrangler. "Your hair." She ran her fingers through his mohawk. "It's longer. Looks good."

Her hands felt good. One touch and his body heated with need. "Don't change the subject." He lowered his voice.

"And when did you get your nose pierced?" He grabbed her hand as she reached out to touch his nose ring. He couldn't handle another caress.

"Hey." Dani's voice grabbed their attention as she ran toward them. "I have your shoes." She dangled the red strappy stilettos from her finger.

Mel trotted to Dani, welcoming her with a hug. "I love you."

"I know, Mellie." She patted Mel's head. "I know."

Joe stood with his arms crossed, watching the two women. Even stupidly drunk, Mel was cute. He'd never seen her this intoxicated before. This wasn't his Melody. "You had one job," Joe scolded Dani. "Keep her off the bar."

Melody turned slowly toward him, flames burning in her hazel eyes. "You don't get to tell me what to do, Rock Star." She staggered up to him. "I'm a big girl." She poked his chest with her index finger. "I've had a really shitty day —one I'd like to forget. This is not her fault."

"You could've had a worse day if I hadn't gotten here when I did. Touchy-feely biker dude wanted more than a dance. And he didn't look like the kind of guy who would ask permission."

"What biker?" Melody snorted.

"The one wanting to kick my ass."

"You mean the one right over there?" Dani pointed to the front of the parking lot.

"Shit." This dude didn't know when to quit. "Melody, get in the Jeep. I'm taking you home." He opened the passenger door, and Mel quickly climbed in. "Dani, where's your car?" he asked as he jogged to the driver's side.

"Right here." Dani pointed to the red sports car next to his Jeep.

"Get in, lock the doors, and get the hell out of here. I'll be right behind you."

Joe turned over the ignition as Dani left the parking lot. He gunned it out of the lot before the biker could get his buddies.

He glanced in the rearview mirror, making sure they weren't being followed. "Jesus Christ." He exhaled in relief when he made the next turn without a single motorcycle in pursuit.

Mel peeked out the back window. "I don't see him."

They looked at each other and burst into laughter. Not even twenty-four hours home and trouble had found them. "Just like the old days."

"Welcome home, Joe," she snickered.

He leaned back in the seat, relieved. A high-speed car chase wasn't on his bucket list.

It was an hour's drive from the Sunset Strip to Santa Monica, where Mel lived, not too far from her father's mansion in Lobo Canyon. He'd taken the twisting desert road through the canyon so many times he could drive it with his eyes closed.

Mel leaned her head back against the headrest, looking out the window. "I'm sorry I almost got your ass kicked tonight. It's been an awful day."

Joe put his hand on her leg and gave it a light squeeze. "So, what happened?"

"You know I've been working really hard to make the LA Orchestra."

"Yeah, you made it through to the last audition."

There was silence.

Dread came over him. She didn't have to say it—she didn't make it. He understood her disappointment. He'd felt the claws of rejection ripping at his soul. God knows, Grace-fall had had their share. "I know it's a bad blow, but this isn't the end."

She turned her head with tears in her eyes. "It was my dream. I sacrificed everything for that one chance, and I blew it."

Joe choked up as he watched a tear roll down her cheek. He'd do anything to make her happy. Even use his celebrity influence and call the head director at the orchestra. One call and she'd have her dream. But he valued his life more; she'd kill him if she ever found out. "Don't be so hard on yourself. You'll make it. It's just not your time."

"And." Irritation filled her tone as she sat up. "I can't even keep a boyfriend. Apparently, I don't know how to love." Unsteady in her seat, she pointed at herself. "Me...I don't know anything about love."

"What are you talking about?"

"I got dumped today, too."

"What?! Brad dumped you on the last day of auditions?"

Her brows pinched together. "Who's Brad? I was talking about Drew!"

"Drew? What the hell? When did you get back together with that douchebag?"

"I told you three months ago."

Three months ago? Either he'd chosen to ignore the fact she had been with another guy or time on the road had gotten away from him. Their lives had been crazy, but he should have been there for her.

Joe glanced at her. He couldn't imagine anyone leaving her. She was the whole package—intelligent, kind-hearted, and gorgeous. "Drew is a douchebag. I've told you that."

Joe pulled into the cobblestone driveway and parked. The two-story, Spanish tiled roof home was exactly as he remembered. Especially the breathtaking view of the Valley. He had fond memories of them sitting on the back balcony gazing across the mountain and talking about life. It was the drive home he hated, where he kicked himself every time for not telling Mel his true feelings. The timing had never been right...until now.

Gracefall had rocketed to the top, and he wanted to share his success with her.

She turned to him and glared. The moon illuminated her face, making her more beautiful than before. "Why are you always right? It's annoying."

He shrugged. "I can't help it. I call bullshit when I see it. Drew is bullshit."

Her face paled. "I feel sick."

"No—No—No! Not in the Jeep." He hopped out like his ass was on fire and rushed to the passenger side to help Mel down. "No vomiting in the Jeep."

"I'm going to be sick." She rushed over to the wispy bed of grass next to the driveway. She bent over, and he held her hair back right before all hell broke loose. Being in a rock band on the road with lots of alcohol...yeah, he'd seen his share of vomit.

He leaned over. "Hey, you okay?"

She stood up and nodded as she wiped her mouth. She handed him her purse. "My keys are in the front pocket."

Fumbling through, he found them and unlocked the door. On their way to the bedroom, he turned on the lights and then helped her to bed. "Stay here."

She flopped back on the bed. "Joe Grace, the rock star." She laughed. "At least one of us made their dreams come true."

He returned with an oversized t-shirt. "Here, put this on and get into bed. You need to sleep it off."

She staggered to her feet. "My head is spinning."

"That's what three Mind Erasers will do to you."

"Four," she corrected.

"Four?" He threw the shirt over his shoulder and amused himself by watching her fumble with the buttons of her silk blouse. "Need help?"

Her arms flopped down by her side. "I give up."

He picked up where she'd left off. As he unbuttoned her blouse, his fingertips brushed against the swell of her breasts. He flinched at the unintentional contact, but the black lacey bra was killing him. Fuck, she felt good.

She gazed up at him. Her friendly expression, the one he was used to, had turned into desire. Was she feeling the way he was?

He narrowed in on her mouth. Full, pink lips drew him in and beckoned to be kissed just like he'd fantasized many times, but never had the nerve to execute. Make no mistake, he'd never been afraid to make the first move, but with Mel things were different. They were friends.

She took the shirt from his shoulder. "I can take it from here."

He cleared his throat. "Yep."

She began to remove her top, and he quickly turned around. Watching her undress would be his undoing.

"Always the gentleman," she joked.

He heard the white leather short shorts hit the floor, and he swallowed hard. Why did this bother him so much? They were friends. That's all.

She stood behind him, her body pressed against his. With one hand on his shoulder for balance, she whispered in his ear, "You can turn around now."

Keeping himself in check, he turned around. Fuck yeah! She was beautiful, staring up at him with big hazel eyes. He played with her hair, bringing it over her shoulders, because if he didn't keep his hands innocently busy in those blonde locks, they'd be on her ass. He cleared his throat. "Bed. Now." He didn't mean for it to sound like a growl, but there was some serious crossing-the-friendship-line shit going on in his head.

He pulled back the sheets, and she slipped into the bed without protest. He leaned over and kissed her forehead. "Get some rest."

As he got up, she pulled on his shirt. "Don't go. Stay with me, please."

The plea in her voice tugged on his heart. She'd had the worst day of her life and needed a friend. Of course, he should stay. He had no intentions of leaving her alone like this. "Yeah, I can stay. I'll be on the couch if you need me."

She pulled back the sheets, inviting him in her bed.

There were a million reasons why he should say no, but only one good reason to say yes—she needed him. He sat down and pulled off his boots. "I'll stay on one condition."

"And what's that?"

He slipped under the covers. "Keep your hands to yourself."

Her laughter warmed his heart. "Yes, sir."

He put his arm around her, and she snuggled close, laying her head on his chest. "Why can't I find someone like you to fall in love with?"

God, if she only knew. "Because I'm one of a kind, baby."

She playfully slapped his chest. "Seriously," she yawned. "I have the worst taste in men."

"I wouldn't give Drew another thought. He's an idiot for letting you go."

There was silence, and for a moment, he thought she'd gone to sleep.

"Joe."

"Mel."

"I won't remember any of this in the morning, will I?"

"Not a thing, baby." He soothed her, brushing her hair off her forehead with his fingers.

"I love you, Joe Grace."

Drunk with happiness, he couldn't believe what she had said. Many times, he'd wanted to tell her the same thing but was too chickenshit. He sobered quickly as he reminded himself that she was the drunk one—she didn't know what she was saying. But part of him wanted to believe it and say it back. He licked his lips and readied himself to confess. "I..."

A soft snore escaped her.

"What the..." He looked down. She'd passed out.

He exhaled. There was a god, and he had been saved from making a huge mistake. Yes, he loved her too, but now wasn't the time to tell her. Besides, they were friends, nothing more.

3

The sound of the blender pulsed in Melody's head as she rolled over in bed. Her mouth was dry, and she smelled like vodka. Wait. What? She sat up, and her head spun. Who was in her house?

She stumbled out of bed and grabbed her gray terrycloth robe. On her way out of the bedroom, she tripped over something by the bed. Through blurry vision, a pair of men's black boots came into focus. "Joe?"

She remembered Dani taking her to the bar, but damn if she knew how she'd gotten home. Through the fog of last night, she recalled Joe at the bar. She'd been excited to see him. Yes, he'd been there. He must have taken her home last night.

She padded through the living room to the kitchen. Every step amplified the thumping in her head as though Godzilla was wreaking havoc in her brain.

"Hey, look what the cat dragged in." Joe turned around, and she froze. No shirt, jeans riding low on his hips. When did he become so sexy? His blond hair was pulled back high on his head—the sides shaved. His beard was lighter, matching the highlights streaked through his hair.

But what got her the most—his steel-gray eyes.

A small gold ring pierced his nose. That was new. Black and gray skulls and skeletons in various designs were tattooed down his muscular arms and across his broad chest. Her eyes narrowed in on a beautiful Celtic cross over his heart. She'd never seen it before, and it was the only one that had any hint of color. Inside the cross, intricate lines entangled together forming a word, but from this far away she couldn't make it out. As she took in the ink, the thought of finding and tracing every single tattoo crossed her mind. He was like a life-size find-the-hidden-objects game. Now wouldn't that be fun?

Fun?

She shook her head. Naughty thoughts weren't allowed. Growing up with musicians, piercings and tattoos had never been a novel thing. But something had changed, and here she was curious, wanting to play Seek and Find on Joe's body. Wanting to trace every single tat with her tongue.

"Sit down. I made you my own hangover remedy that's been proven many times to cure all ailments. Just ask Dylan."

She sat down on the barstool at the kitchen island as he handed her what looked like a light-brown smoothie. She brought the glass to her nose.

"Oh, no." Joe pushed the glass away from her nose. "Don't smell it, just drink it."

Even though it looked like a flaming-hot mess, she'd drink anything to make her head stop throbbing and her stomach stop flip-flopping. She took a sip and almost threw up in her mouth. "What is this? It's horrible."

"Trust me, keep drinking."

She took another sip, and Joe tipped the glass, making her drink it all.

Protesting the entire time, she finished the smoothie. She wiped her mouth with the back of her hand and wrinkled her nose. "That's nasty, Joe. Is that what all the rock stars drink now? I've never seen my dad drink such a concoction."

He laughed. "Yep. You'll thank me later."

He turned back around, attending to something sizzling on the stove. "Hope you're hungry."

"How can I possibly eat anything after that smoothie from hell? Are you going to tell me what's in it? I think I tasted banana."

He nodded. "That and coconut water, peanut butter, and pickle juice. You didn't have any ginger, so I had to improvise with pickle juice."

She was sorry she asked.

He placed a plate of eggs, toast, and fruit in front of her. "You need to eat. And make sure you drink a lot of water today." He positioned his hands on the counter in front of her and leaned in. The muscles in his arms bulged against his weight. He was strong, and by all that was holy, he looked sexy standing in her kitchen, cooking her breakfast.

The air between them disappeared, making it hard to breathe. What was wrong with her? Joe was her friend, and she didn't date musicians, especially rock stars.

He tipped his chin toward the plate, breaking the spell she was under. "Eat."

She picked up a fork and dug into the scrambled eggs. Joe remembered how she liked her eggs. "So, what brings you back to Cali? And why didn't you call me? I would have picked you up from the airport."

"Yeah, I sort of freaked out a bit." He pushed off the counter, giving them some space.

"What do you mean?"

"I hadn't talked to you in a while, and I knew Brad was in the picture, and you were practicing for the orchestra."

"Drew," she corrected. "His name is Drew."

"Right."

"That's no excuse. We promised each other our friendship always comes first."

He rubbed the back of his neck. "To be honest, I felt you slipping away."

Her heart sank. She'd been so engrossed in making the orchestra auditions she'd almost lost the most important thing in her life—Joe's friendship. "I'm sorry. I should have called you more."

Joe shrugged. "I'm not blaming you. I just freaked and had to wait to call."

"So," she prodded for more information. "Obviously, you called someone. You found me. Did you call my dad?"

"No. Actually, I called you, and Dani answered."

"Oh." Embarrassed, she avoided his gaze and stabbed a strawberry with her fork. God only knew what she'd done last night.

"I called to tell you Gracefall is headlining a four-month, twenty-six show tour. Whiplash is opening for us."

"What!" She dropped her fork. "You're headlining?"

"Yep." The biggest smile spread across his lips.

She jumped off the barstool and rushed him with a huge hug. "I'm so proud of you. You made it, baby."

He hugged her tight. "I want you to come with me."

She pulled back, not believing what she'd heard. "Joe." She shook her head.

"Wait before you say no. I've been giving it a lot of

thought. I think it would be good for you to leave town for the summer and clear your head. Besides, I know you love to travel."

"I do, but not on a tour bus with crazy rock musicians." Growing up, she'd been on many tours with her father. She knew the scene—the women, the drugs, the parties. "I will not tag along on the tour bus like some groupie. No way."

Joe exhaled, frustrated. "You know it's not like that." He stepped forward and took her hands in his. "You're the only person I want to share this experience with."

He gazed longingly into her eyes, and she swore her knees went weak. A man like Joe had *The Look*. That seductive stare-down, gaze filled with sexual electricity. It's the look all mothers warned their daughters about. It's the look that made good girls do bad things—pure rock star.

"I can't." She walked away while she still could and returned to her breakfast.

Joe stood across from her. "Give me one good reason."

She paused. Nothing was keeping her here except working at her father's music studio, teaching cello. "My students."

"I'm sure your father can find a sub."

"Let's say he does. I can't take the summer off."

"Why?"

"I have bills to pay."

Joe stroked his whiskered chin as he studied her briefly. "You're hired."

"What?"

"You can be our tour manager."

"Are you insane? That would not go over well with the band's management."

"No, and I don't give a fuck about what management says. You'd be perfect. You know the ins and outs of being on the road. You've been to most arenas and major venues throughout North America. You know these places like the back of your hand. And you are the only one on the bus who can balance a budget."

She shook her head. "I can't."

Her phone vibrated as a text message came through. She picked up the pink-cased cell. There was a text from Dani. Thank God her bestie had amazing timing. She really didn't want to have this conversation with Joe. "It's Dani checking up on me."

Dani: Hey, girl! How ya feeling?

Melody replied with a green sick-faced emoji.

Dani: That bad, huh?"

Melody: I'll never drink again.

A gray incoming text bubble pulsed for a while. To avoid Joe, she pretended to text. Seriously, what was he thinking? She couldn't just pack up and leave. Besides, she had no interest in babysitting a bunch of rock stars.

However, she'd known all the members of Gracefall well. They were a good group of guys—wild, but a hell of a band. Living with them on a bus, now that would try her last nerve. Then there was Joe. Given the way she'd been thinking about him just a few minutes ago, it would be safer for their friendship if she didn't go.

The text came through. A video? She tapped on the sideways triangle. "Oh my..." she placed her hand over her mouth as she watched herself dancing on top of the bar.

"What?" Joe grabbed her phone. "Oh yeah, this went down last night." He belted out in laughter.

Humiliated, she hid her face in her hands. "Please tell me I kept my clothes on."

"Yep, but you gave everyone an outstanding show."

She peeked between her fingers at him. A sexy grin

spread across his lips as he watched the video. Did he actually like what he saw?

She reached across the table and grabbed her phone back. "Give me that." She fumbled, trying to shut the video down when another text came up.

Dani: Sorry, but not sorry!

Melody: DO NOT POST THIS ON SOCIAL MEDIA!!!!

Dani: Then go with Joe on tour. You deserve a vacation!

Wait. What? How did Dani know about Joe and the tour?

Dani: Don't ask me how I know. I'll never tell.

She added a wink emoji.

Dani: If your ass isn't on the tour bus, Tiny Dancer goes viral.

She looked over the phone at Joe. "Did you put her up to this?"

His brows creased. "Up to what?"

She handed him the phone. "Blackmail."

He read the messages. "I have no idea how she found out. I checked in with the band this morning. I mentioned it to—"

She cocked a brow. "Dylan."

"Son of a bitch," Joe rubbed the back of his neck. "I didn't think Dylan and Dani would hook up last night. I assumed she'd gone home after we left the bar."

"If she knew you were in town, you know where she spent last night." She slid off the barstool and brought her plate to the sink. Everyone saw through Dani's hard exterior —her weakness had always been Dylan, even though she knew she was only a booty call.

After drying her hands, she turned back around, and there was Joe standing way too close with his smoldering rock star stare. "What?"

"Don't avoid the question."

"I didn't. I said no." She crossed her arms over her chest, creating a much-needed barrier between them.

"You have to go. You can't let Dani blackmail you."

"She's bluffing. Dani would never do something like that —or would she?" Frustrated and flustered, she shook her head. "Not the point. I can handle it."

"Come on, Mel. Don't make me beg. Ever since we were kids, we'd dreamed of seeing the world. Remember our spot at your dad's place?"

How could she forget? Many times, after cello practice, she'd met Joe under the huge live oak where they would lay looking up at the stars and listen to music Joe had saved on his iPod. God, she missed those simpler times. "I remember you playing Shinedown, "If You Only Knew," like a million times."

A smile crept across his lips like he'd remembered, too. "Remember what I told you when Dylan and I formed Gracefall?"

She did. "You told me we'd tour the world together."

"I meant it. You and me, traveling the world."

"You make it sound so simple, but it's not. You're missing one fine detail, the rock and roll lifestyle. Joe, I lived in that fantasy world, watched it destroy my parents. I can't do that to our friendship."

"We're nothing like your parents. We actually get along."

Her lips curved up into a smile. He was right. She couldn't remember a time when she'd tired of him. As kids, he was always at her dad's house. The only time she didn't see him was when her mother had visitation. "When do you need an answer?"

"I leave in three days, so as soon as possible."

Melody took him in, tattoos and all, as she decided what

to do. There was too much at stake here. She couldn't just leave. Playing for the orchestra was her dream, and she couldn't achieve that traveling with a rock band.

Then there was their friendship. They had promised each other that their friendship would always come first. They had never crossed the line, even though she'd wanted him to a million times.

"I need to talk to my dad before I commit to anything."

She watched the biggest smile come across his face, reminding her of the boy sitting under the live oak tree, unknowingly stealing her heart. "That's fair." He played off the excitement, but she knew deep down what he was feeling, because she was feeling it too. She just needed her dad to talk her out of it.

4

With the top down on her two-seater sportscar, Melody drove the winding road to her father's house. Today had been much better than yesterday. No more hangover. The sun was out warming her skin, her hair was down and blowing in the wind, and the radio pumped out her favorite tunes. The morning had been perfect, except when she had been pondering over Joe's offer. Should she stay? Should she go? She'd even made a list of pros and cons like she had for every big life decision. Pros: she liked to travel, she wouldn't mind spending time with Joe and catching up, managing a tour would be a good experience. Cons: rock and roll lifestyle, the possibility of ruining her friendship with Joe.

She huffed and gripped the steering wheel, no closer to making up her mind. She knew the responsible answer, yet a part of her wanted to be with Joe. It was great seeing him again, even though she'd felt a shift in their relationship.

As if it was a sign, Gracefall came on the radio. It warmed her heart knowing Joe had made his dream come true, and she was his biggest fan. She turned the sound up, remembering a time when Joe couldn't hold a beat. She'd never told him how she would sneak down to the lesson studio and secretly watch him play. The scrawny, scruffy thirteen-year-old intrigued her, even at a young age. As innocent as it was, there was something about Joe Grace that drew her in.

She pulled into the main house entrance and punched in the gate code to her father's estate. Black wrought-iron gates opened with a groan, welcoming her home. It had been a while since she'd driven the winding paved driveway to her father's home. Driving down it now confirmed that lately she'd neglected the people around her so she could eat, sleep, and breathe acing her audition. Disappointment knotted in her chest. She'd spent a relentless number of hours practicing the perfect cello piece that had showcased her talent, and now she had absolutely nothing to show for it except a few new calluses on her fingers and lost time with her friends and family.

Tucked behind gates and nestled under a canopy of trees sat The God of Thunder's contemporary Mediter-ranean-style mansion on twenty acres. As she pulled up to the house, Joe's Jeep was parked in the driveway.

Great, Joe had beat her to it. She'd bet he was in there right now persuading her dad, telling him that managing a tour would be an excellent experience for her. She pulled down the sun visor and did a quick makeup check in the tiny rectangular mirror before getting out of the car. As she made her way to the front door, she ran her fingers through her tousled hair and readjusted her top for the second time. Realizing what she was doing, she paused at the door. *Really, Mel? Primping for Joe?*

She shook off the thought and went inside.

Anita, her father's housekeeper, was pruning a huge

arrangement of tropical plants that sat on a circular table in the middle of the foyer, which was big enough to be another room. She never understood why her father needed such a mammoth house when he lived alone. Since he was deemed a god, she guessed he had to live like one.

Anita's mouth dropped open as she saw her. "Meloda!" She raced toward her with arms wide open.

"Anita!" Melody hugged her tight. She'd known Anita practically all her life, and she was like a second mother to her. Her words of wisdom throughout the years had been a godsend.

Anita took a step back, examined her, and tsk-tsked. "You look thin. Come, I'll fix you breakfast." She took her hand, leading her to the kitchen.

She knew better than to refuse—it would be an insult. Anita was happiest when people were enjoying her food. "Have you seen my dad?"

"Sí, Mr. Leo is reading the newspaper at the dining room table." She looked over her shoulder and smiled. "Joe is here."

Joe's charm had no bounds. He'd even bewitched Anita. "Yes, I saw his Jeep out front."

Melody walked into the dining area where four arched doors along the back wall were open, giving her a familiar view of the pool. Just in front of the doors, the God of Thunder sat cross-legged at the head of his vintage Mediterranean-style wood table wearing his bath robe, black socks, and leather house slippers. Melody smiled. If only his fans could see him now.

Leo looked up over his reading glasses. "Hey, Sugar Plum," he greeted her as she walked over and kissed his cheek.

"Morning." She snagged a strawberry off his plate and

took a bite. "Joe," she greeted him with a suspicious glare. "So." Melody sat down next to her dad across from Joe. "I'm assuming, dad, you already know why I'm here."

Leo ruffled the newspaper as he turned the page. He cocked his head back reading the fine print, acting as if everything was right in the world. "I haven't a clue, sweetheart."

She turned her attention on Joe. "You didn't tell him?"

"Tell me what?" Her father shot her a concerned look over his glasses.

She stared at Joe from across the table. *He hadn't told him.*

Anita came into the room holding two plates piled with eggs, fruit, and her famous Pan de Queso, placing one in front her and the other in front of Joe. Melody watched him pop a piece of cheese bread into his mouth. His eyes rolled back in his head. "Anita!" He swallowed. "If you weren't married..."

Anita blushed and patted him on the shoulder. "You're too young for me. Besides, I don't have time to teach a pup new tricks." She smiled, then left the room with a sashay of the hips.

Melody kept her glare on Joe as he looked up from his plate. "What? I didn't say a word. I'm just here visiting. No other motives."

"Yeah, right."

Leo folded his paper and placed it on the table. "Are you two going to tell me what's going on?"

Melody turned to her father. "Joe wants me to manage Gracefall's summer tour."

The room fell silent.

"I mean, that's crazy, right, dad?" She prayed her father was on her side, but when he didn't come unglued at Joe, she knew he was on Joe's side.

Joe slowly got up from his chair. "I should go." He grabbed his plate. "I'll ask Anita for a to-go bag."

"No way, Joe Grace." Melody pointed at him. "Don't you dare go far. This isn't over."

"Yes, ma'am."

She waited until Joe left the room to continue. She looked at her dad, who looked as if he had to a million thoughts running through his head but didn't know how to communicate them.

"Dad, tell me I'm right. This is crazy. I can't just leave for the summer. I have commitments."

"Like what?"

She did a quick mental check on her pros and cons list, purposely leaving out the pros. "My cello students."

"I can find a sub."

"Well, I have bills to pay."

"You'll make plenty of money managing the tour to cover your bills. Anita and I can take care of your place until you get back."

"My dream is the orchestra. I can't throw all that hard work away."

"You have time to take a break before auditions next fall."

"Dad, I can't." She couldn't lose focus on her dreams. The orchestra was her life.

Leo straightened in his chair and removed his glasses. His demeanor was serious, which wasn't good for her argument. Did he actually think this was a good idea? "Sugar Plum, I think you're missing the true meaning of Joe inviting you on tour."

"What do you mean?"

Leo sighed deeply. "You don't know, do you? That boy

has been in love with you since the first day he laid eyes on you."

Melody sank back into the chair. Had it been that obvious? No, it couldn't have been. Whatever he'd seen between her and Joe was only wishful thinking on his part. "Dad, we're friends. That's it. Besides, I'm not falling for the sex, drugs, and rock and roll fantasy life. I've seen what it does to a relationship. No thanks."

A haunting shadow crept across Leo's face. "Mel, I screwed up. That's why your mother hates me."

A knot formed in her chest. He'd never talked about the problems he had with her mother, let alone admitted he was to blame. She'd learned about most of their issues through her mother or she'd witnessed it herself.

"Let me be clear, you and Joe are nothing like me and your mother. Look, you and Joe can deny it all you want, but it's fate. I see how he looks at you."

"Stop." The recent attraction she felt toward Joe had knocked her off kilter. She was thinking about him in ways that would make the devil blush. And seeing him again had brought back beautiful memories. But he would be gone soon, and that was for the best.

"Fine." Leo threw his hands up. "I still think this job will be a good experience for you. You're smart, you're organized, you know what it's like to manage a tour, and you have rock and roll in your veins."

Mentally, she went through her list.

She knew she could do the job. That was a no-brainer.

She couldn't deny she loved traveling.

She knew all the guys in band, and most importantly she got along with them.

She really wanted to test the limits of Joe's friendship— see where things would go.

God, what was she doing? She should have burned that damn list.

"I don't know. Everything is happening too fast."

"I think you do know."

"I came here today so you would talk me out of going."

Her dad gave her a knowing smile. "Sugar Plum, I knew as soon as you walked in here you were Gracefall's new tour manger."

A twinge of excitement pulsed in her chest. What was she getting herself into?

"I should go find Joe and tell him." She got up and hugged her dad. "Thanks for the talk."

"Yep." He went back to his paper. "That's what I'm here for."

~

*J*oe leaned against the huge live oak outside, waiting for Mel. This would be the first place she'd look for him. Being back in California in Leo's house brought a mix of emotions. He'd only been back once since he graduated from high school, and that was to take Mel to her senior prom. A lot had happened since then. Mel had graduated from college. He'd set out on the road to prove to the world that Gracefall would be successful, and they had been. Three bestselling albums and a fourth racing to the top.

And Mel had been there every step of the way. She'd supported him and the band when no one else had. Every time they had a show in town, she was there with Dani in the front row. Seeing her singing along to songs he'd written was the best feeling ever.

If she only knew that everything he had, he wanted to

share with her. Not like he was going to tell her, though. He was in the permanent friend zone. Somehow, he'd find a way to break through.

He'd never felt worthy of Melody. A trailer park kid had no business dreaming about loving a rock and roll princess, and a struggling musician couldn't provide for one either. But now, he was neither. The timing was perfect. He had fortune and fame and could give her everything she was accustomed to.

He looked at the green hedge that ran down the property, separating the mansion from the maintenance quarters. Beyond the wall of greenery, he could barely see the roof of the maintenance shed. Dark memories threatened to surface of a time he pretended didn't exist. Locked up tight, his monsters were real. But none of that mattered now.

"Hey." He turned around to find Melody walking toward him. "Thought I'd find you out here." Her smile was like magic. Didn't matter what kind of mood he was in, her smile shined straight onto his soul.

"I needed to take a walk after eating all that food." He couldn't tell her the real reason why he was out here. It was their spot, but it was much more than that to him. "So?"

"Well, looks as if I'm your new tour manager."

Excitement breached his typical, steady Joe demeanor. "Fuck yeah!" He picked her up and twirled her around. Her laughter and her arms around his neck felt damn good. He didn't want to let her go.

He placed her back on her feet, and they both quickly reclaimed their composure. "Tomorrow I'll introduce you to our tour crew."

"Don't get too excited, Rock Star. I haven't been hired yet."

"Yes, you have. I said so."

Melody sat down, resting her back against the tree. Her smile gone.

"Hey, what's wrong?" Joe joined her under the tree.

She shrugged. "I guess I'm a little nervous."

"Melody, you know you can do the job."

"That's not it."

Joe had a good guess what was on her mind. They had a similar conversation about their friendship changing when he'd left her the first time he went on tour. She was entering her first year of college, and he was scared she'd fall in love with some college boy before he had a chance to prove his love to her. Though he never told her his true feelings, they made a pact that their friendship would always come first.

"Hey." He playfully shoulder bumped her. "Our friendship is strong. If we can survive long distance, we can sure as hell can survive living on a bus together for the summer."

"You're right." Her mood lightened. "I'm looking forward to getting away for a while with my best friend."

Dagger straight to his heart. Little did she know, things were about to change between them.

"So, what are your plans until we leave?" She tucked her hair behind her ear. "Are you staying with your mom?"

"No, with Dylan." Joe hated lying, but he couldn't tell her he'd shacked up with Leo last night, and he wasn't about to explain why he hadn't seen the demon bitch. The road had been his home for so long. Maybe after the tour he'd have a good reason to stick around.

"Have you told your mom about the good news? I'm sure she'll be excited that both her sons are headliners."

She was probing again in her nonchalant way. She was curious, he got that. He'd never talked about his mother or living in the trailer park. Being friends for as long as they had and not meeting his mom had led to questions and a lie he'd take to the grave.

"She's out of the country. Some place in Brazil." Telling Mel all those years ago that his mom was a traveling nurse had been the prefect lie.

"Oh, wow. She really has a passion for taking care of people."

Yep, crack whore Karen had a passion...for the wrong people.

"I have no plans." Joe crossed his arms and leaned his head toward hers. "Though we do need to get you packed. We have to be on the bus Friday morning."

"Shouldn't take me long to pack."

"I want to introduce you to the tour crew, so I'll be at your place at ten thirty tomorrow morning. Clef Tonic is an hour drive."

She laid her head on his shoulder. "I can't believe we're doing this."

He reached over and held her hand, something he'd never thought about doing in the past. But right now it felt right. She glanced up at him with questioning eyes. "Don't worry," he comforted her. "This is meant to be."

On so many levels, this was meant to be.

5

*I*n awe, Melody took in the fourteen-story high-rise as Joe pulled into the parking garage. Clef Tonic Records was located across the street from the Sunset Strip. On the west side of the building, facing the Strip, where all the music clubs were located, a twelve-story art mural dedicated to big name rock bands that had signed with the record company covered the floor-to-ceiling windows. It was a reminder to all the aspiring rock bands paying their rock and roll dues that dreams do come true. This place was the Holy Grail to musicians.

Joe parked his Jeep and shut off the engine. "Are you ready to meet the crew?"

Melody had no idea how to dress for the occasion. It wasn't a job interview, but she knew entering a record company with the last name of Sterling would mean all eyes were going to be on her. She pulled down the visor and made sure that no loose tendrils had fallen from her twisted ponytail.

"Melody, you look great. Remember, this is rock and roll. You're already overdressed."

"Really?" Melody looked down at her white blouse and black trousers. She'd changed at least three times this morning. She was overthinking the whole thing, but first impressions were important. Being the daughter of Leo Sterling had taught her that. "I thought this was business casual attire."

Amused, Joe shook his head as he got out of the car. She watched him walk around the front of the Jeep before opening her door. Since when did he open car doors for her? He held her hand, helping her out of the Jeep. "Stop worrying. Everyone will love you."

They got into the elevator, and Joe punched in the floor number. While her heart hammered in her chest, Joe was cool as usual, leaning against the back of the elevator. She took in a couple deep breaths. She could do this—she was a Sterling.

As the elevator ascended, she felt Joe's eyes on her and glanced over her shoulder. A big smile painted his lips. "What?"

"You're cute when you're nervous."

"I'm not nervous," she lied. "I got this."

"Right," he snickered.

What was she really nervous about? She knew the music industry and knew how to deal with the people running the show. Could it be that Joe was rattling her cage a bit? Holding her hand, opening the door, the tender way he looked at her? Most definitely.

The elevator stopped, and the doors opened on the twelfth floor to a spacious central meeting area with floor-to-ceiling windows. In the distance, through the haze in the sky, she saw the LA skyline. No matter how many times she'd seen the city, at this height it took her breath away.

Joe put his hand on the small of her back and led her

into the office. A chick with bright-pink hair, heavy black eyeliner, and symmetrical cheek piercings that looked like metal dimples greeted them from the receptionist's desk. "Hey, Joe."

"Hey, Cherry. Where's Robyn?"

"I'm filling in for her today. But don't worry, I got the tour schedule you asked for. I even put it in a neat little binder." She handed it to him.

"You're the best, Cherry."

"I know. I know." She motioned for him to keep praising.

"So, Cherry, this is Melody Sterling. She'll be managing our summer tour."

Cherry shook her hand. "Rock on."

By the girl's passive reaction, it was obvious Cherry had been too young to recognize her last name. "Nice to meet you."

"Melody, this is Cherry Lane, my personal assistant. You two should swap numbers. She's sitting this tour out but will be handling my schedule from here."

"Already done." Cherry pointed at the binder in Joe's hand. "It's on the front page along with Kimmy's."

The phone rang and Cherry went back to work.

Joe handed Melody the binder. "So, this is the tour itinerary. It has everything you'll need: important numbers, schedules, accommodations, and venue contacts. Go through it. If you're missing anything, let Davidson know."

"Who's Davidson?"

"He's our band manager."

"Okay." She was taken aback witnessing Joe the Rock Star at work. Since when did Joe have an assistant?

"Hey, Joseph." A man in his late fifties with a long, scruffy, graying beard and tattoos approach them.

"Sal!" They clapped each other's shoulders. "I'm so glad

you're here. This is Melody Sterling, my tour manger. Mel, this Sal. He's the captain of the ship."

Stars twinkled in his eyes as he shook her hand. "Leo Sterling's baby girl. The pleasure is all mine."

Melody smiled.

"I drove The Wicked tour for your dad years ago. Whew! What a party that was."

"I'm sure it was."

Sal kept looking at her in awe, which made her feel a bit uncomfortable. "Hot damn, Baby Sterling will be managing Gracefall's tour." He reached in his back pocket. "You're going to need these and pray you'll never have to use them." He handed her a pair of pink fuzzy handcuffs.

"Handcuffs?" Confused, she held them by the chain connecting the cuffs. She raised a brow to Joe.

"Not for me, but I'm always willing to experiment." He wiggled his brows.

"In my experience," Sal added, "there's always that one band member that needs more policing than the others. I think you know which one."

Sal was right. She knew which Gracefall member she'd have to keep her eye on. "Thanks, Sal. I'll keep that in mind." She tucked the cuffs inside the binder.

"Tell your dad Sal says hi, and I'll see ya on the bus Friday morning." As he walked away, he shouted, "And don't be late."

*M*elody playfully glared at Joe. "Please tell me I won't have to use the cuffs on Dylan."

He put his arm around her, leading her down the hallway. "I'm making no promises."

They laughed.

As they walked down the hallway, she looked at the walls covered in photos of musicians from throughout the decade. If she looked longer, she bet she'd find one with her father in it. Yep, first row, third picture.

A group of five rockers with tattoos and piercings led by a frazzled woman with raven hair walked toward them.

"Hi, Joe," the woman greeted them, then turned her attention to Melody. "You must be Melody Sterling. Kimmy Anderson." Melody shook her hand. "I'm Gracefall and Whiplash's public relations representative. God help me."

"Nice to meet you." Melody eyed the guys behind Kimmy. They had to be Whiplash.

"Joe fucking Grace." A man with long brown hair who looked like he came straight out of the movie *Rockstar* bumped shoulders with Joe. "I haven't seen your ugly ass in ages."

"Well, looks like you'll be seeing a lot of it this summer. Welcome to the tour, brother."

"Dude." Another guy with black shoulder-length hair and a matching goatee came forward and shook Joe's hand. "This summer is going to be epic."

"For sure." Joe looked at Melody. "Hey, guys, this is Melody Sterling. She's my new tour manager."

"No fucking way," she heard someone in the back say. A teal-haired, petite woman who could pass as a mermaid pushed her way forward. "As in Leo Sterling, The God of Thunder?"

"That would be my dad." Melody held her hand out but was greeted with a hug.

"I love your dad. Taught me everything I know."

"So, you're the drummer of the band?"

"Yep, I'm Misti. This is Devin." She pointed at the guy with long brown hair. "That's..." she scratched her chin as she eyed the guy with the goatee. "What's your name again?"

"Fucking funny, Stixx."

"That's right. Adam Winter." Misti laughed.

Adam raised his hand and greeted Melody with rock horns.

"I hate to break up the introductions," Kimmy interrupted. "We have a radio promo thing downtown." She looked at her watch. "And we're late."

"Let Devin drive." Misti said. "We'll be there in ten minutes tops."

"Hell, yeah! I feel the need." He raised his hand, presenting rock horns. "The need for speed."

Inwardly Melody rolled her eyes at the *Top Gun* reference. Devin was definitely the lead singer.

Joe and Melody continued down the hall.

"It's going to be a crazy summer, huh?" She looked at Joe.

"With those guys, never a dull moment."

At the end of the hallway there was a glass-walled office. Inside, a well-built and well-put-together man was on the phone, pacing the room in what looked to be an intense argument. She assumed it was Davidson. He saw Joe and waved them in.

The office looked more like an upscale hotel room, minus the bed. A red mahogany desk sat in front of floor-to-ceiling windows where he had a spectacular view of the skyline. Various species of house plants dotted the office, giving it a topical feel. Davidson motioned for them to sit. She took a seat on the teal-green couch that was a shade darker than the rug beneath it.

She opened the binder and flipped through the first couple of pages, which outlined the tour schedule, as Davidson finished his call. Joe stood next to the widows, looking at the city below them. He seemed deep in thought, and she wished she knew what he was thinking. Was he having regrets? She wouldn't take it personally if he was.

"So, what the hell is going on?" Davidson exclaimed as he tossed his cell on the desk. "Why did I have to hear from Big Rick that Melody Sterling is the new tour manager?"

"Well, good morning to you." Joe crossed his arms.

"I'm in no mood for your shit today. I don't like this idea of a woman on the bus twenty-four seven, and I'm not keen on a woman running the show, dig?"

A lump formed in Melody's throat. Joe hadn't talked to management about the job offer. She sank into the couch, wishing it would swallow her whole before Davidson realized she was in the room. Or maybe he did, and he didn't care. Either way, the vibe he was sending out wasn't welcoming.

"Look—" Joe began, but Davidson cut him off.

"No, you look. I'm your manager. I'm in charge. Do you have any idea what you have done? A woman will change the dynamics on the bus. Did you consider that?"

"Davidson, calm—"

"Besides, what credentials does she have? Yes, her father is some big name, but that doesn't mean she can do the job."

"Hold up." Joe strode toward Davidson. "First of all, I am in charge. Gracefall is my band, understand? Second, Melody Sterling is our new tour manager, dig?" he mocked his band manager.

"I'm not paying her so you can have pussy twenty-four seven on the bus."

Before Joe said a word, Melody stood. She'd had enough

of being berated by this guy, who reminded her of a slimy used car salesman. As much as she wanted to lash out, she kept her professional composure. Besides, if she didn't intervene, Joe was totally going to kick this guy's ass.

She straightened her shoulders and approached Davidson. "Melody Sterling." His mood went rigid, yet his eyes looked her over as if shocked she had the balls to approach him. "If you want a resume, I have one." She handed her phone to him with a picture of her standing next to her father holding a Grammy. "Do you need more? I'm sure I have a picture of his wall at home filled with platinum and double-platinum records."

"No, that won't be necessary." He handed her phone back.

"Great. Now that we have that out of the way, there are a few issues with the tour schedule. There's a suitability issue with one of the venues."

"Darlin', I highly doubt that." He snickered.

Melody pulled out the list of venues. "My name is Melody." She handed him the sheet. "I'm sure you're aware that the Helix Stadium in Texas is under construction."

"What are you talking about?" He looked at the list.

"The stadium has been under construction for the past year. There's no way the guys can play there in July. Unless you want them playing on top of rubble."

Davidson's face sobered.

"This will need to be rescheduled. Maybe try Millennium Field?"

"Right." He scratched his head.

"And." She handed him the tour schedule. "You might want to read up on the Federal Motor Carrier Safety Administration 60/70 hours of service regulations. Some of the milage goes over regulations. Those are some hefty fines.

Besides, Sal needs his beauty rest so the band can arrive safely at the venues. Or hire a relief driver."

"Well, looks like you've done your homework, Miss Sterling."

Melody walked over to him and placed the binder on his desk. She pinned him with her best fuck you glare. "Darlin', I lived it."

"Fair enough."

She took a step toward the door. "I'm expecting an updated itinerary waiting for me on the bus tomorrow."

Davidson cleared his throat. "On it."

"Good." She walked toward the door, keeping herself composed.

Joe walked by Davidson on his way out. "I wouldn't fuck with her." He shook his head and snickered. "Davidson, you look like you've just shit yourself."

Melody strode out of Davidson's office to the elevator, trying hard to keep it together. She was coming down from an adrenaline rush, which meant a release of tears were right around the corner. It had been a long time since she'd dealt with people like him. Even though she tried not to allow him to get her, he had.

"Mel." Joe jogged behind her to catch up, but she wasn't stopping until she reached the elevator.

She folded her arms around her stomach for comfort as she waited for the doors to open. "Come on, come on." The door slid open and she rushed in. Her hand shook as she frantically pushed the ground floor button.

"Hey." Joe slipped in just before the door closed. "Mel, what's wrong?"

She looked up, trying to stop the tears from rolling down her cheeks. "That guy is an asshole." Her voice shook.

"Come here." He pulled her into a hug. She laid her

head on his chest and exhaled a shaky breath. "He'll never talk to you like that again, okay?"

Yeah, she doubted that. She nodded since she couldn't talk past the sob forming in her throat. She was more upset at herself for allowing Davidson to rattle her.

Joe's soothing hands rubbed her back in a circular motion, making her feel protected. Melody melted into his embrace, breathing in his familiar scent of sandalwood, and the world melted away. She held him tighter.

"If it makes you feel any better, I thoroughly enjoyed watching you stick it to him. I'm one lucky bastard to have you in my corner."

The elevator stopped with a jolt, breaking her peace. Melody took a step back and wiped her cheeks. She was sure her mascara had run, and she must have looked like a mess. "I'm sorry."

He held her head in his hands. His thumbs brushed away the remaining tears. Her heart skipped a beat as he gazed into her eyes. "There's no need to be sorry. I should have warned you about Davidson."

Completely distracted, she narrowed in on his full lips. What would his kiss taste like? Knowing Joe, black liquorish mixed with whiskey—two of his favorite things. How would his lips feel against her skin? A shiver of desire raced down her spine as she imagined him kissing down her neck and slowly making his way down to her breasts.

Heat flushed her cheeks and she looked away. She cleared her throat. "You think?" She rolled her eyes.

"Seriously, I would never let anyone hurt you. I will have a talk with him."

As she looked into his eyes, something had changed between them—she felt it. He'd been acting differently around her. He'd touched her often. He'd spent more time with her. And if she weren't mistaken, he'd been jealous of Drew.

Were they both considering knocking down the friend zone barrier?

6

*F*riday morning traffic on the freeway was a bitch, especially as Joe pulled onto it and came to an immediate dead stop. *Great, an accident.* He checked his watch. Even with a delay and assuming Dylan would be late, they should make it to the tour bus on time.

He glanced over at Melody sitting in the passenger seat. How in the hell had he pulled it off? Melody, his tour manager? They had the whole summer together—he had the whole summer to show her they were meant to be together. Knowing her reservations about the rock and roll lifestyle, it was going to take some convincing, but he had no doubt by the end of the tour, Melody Sterling would be more than just a friend.

The air conditioner lightly blew her blonde hair, filling his Jeep with her vanilla scent. Her head rested back against the seat. Through her gold aviator sunglasses, he couldn't tell if she had fallen asleep. After a few more glances, it was safe to say she was sleeping—prime time for him to take a longer look.

He couldn't stop his eyes from roaming down her pink

and teal plaid button-down shirt that clung to her breasts down to her short, frayed cutoff jean shorts. Her California sun-kissed legs were stunning. Even better if they were wrapped around his waist.

"Keep your eyes on the road, Rock Star." She turned her head toward him and smiled.

"Sorry." His eyes were back on the road. "I just haven't seen you in a while. I've missed you."

"Yeah, it feels like an eternity since we've spent the night together," she said sarcastically. "Totally craving one of your smoothies of death." She winked.

Yep, he'd missed her sarcasm. "You know what I mean."

"I know." She took a long drink from the water bottle he made her bring. "I'm looking forward to spending time with you. It's the other three I worry about."

"They're harmless."

"Are you sure the guys are okay with me managing the tour?"

"Of course. They know, respect, and trust you. In fact, Mox about lost his shit when I told him about it."

Silence filled the Jeep. He sensed her apprehension. It was understandable. Guys in rock bands had bad reputations. Boredom on the road was the bane of their existence. Parties quickly got out of control. It would take a supernatural act herding the band from city to city in one piece.

Not to mention, collecting money from venue managers could be difficult. Some promoters were assholes. And then there were the roadies. Maybe he didn't think this all the way through.

No, she's a pro. She could handle it. Besides, he'd be right there by her side if she needed help.

"Hey, what is this?" She pulled out a magazine wedged between her seat and the center console. "*DrumBeat Maga-*

zine. And look who's on the cover. Joe Grace from Gracefall." She dangled the magazine, teasing.

"Give me that." He grabbed at the magazine but missed as she pulled it away. "You're not going to read it."

"Oh, yes, I am." She grinned at the cover. "Look at you behind the TAMA Superstar 6 piece." She cocked a brow. "Double bass. My father would be impressed."

Leo Sterling, the God of Thunder, the King of Skin had taught him to play. So yeah, he was proud he'd impressed an icon. Inside, he cringed as she opened to the interview. "I really wish you wouldn't read it."

"Why? Afraid I won't like Joe the Rock Star."

He played it cool. "Go ahead. Knock yourself out."

She gave him the side-eye and smiled. She cleared her throat, then read the interview out loud.

Gracefall is on the fast track to superstardom. Their third album, Surrender to the Unknown, *is an ass-kicking heavy metal good time, proving rock isn't dead.*

Today, Joe Grace, the famously stoic drummer and namesake of Gracefall, is stopping by to talk about the new album.

She glanced at him. "Oh, this is going to be good." She smiled.

DB: Surrender to the Unknown, *by far, is the heaviest album of Gracefall. The drumming rocked my balls off.*

JG: (laughter) Fuck Yeah. (Joe raises his hand a gives me the universal metal horns symbol.)

DB: Songs like "Half-Alive" and "Visiting Darkness," I think, are the heaviest musically and lyrically. You and Dylan are the primary songwriters in the group. What's your writing process?

JG: We've been writing since we were kids. It was a healthy way for us to express our thoughts. (Joe shakes his head.) Dylan comes up with some dark shit. If we're feeling it, we write it down. I'll come up with a beat, Mox comes up with the rhythm,

Tyler comes in with his hard-hitting bassline, and the rest is history.

DB: So, everyone is in on the process?

JG: Yeah. I mean, we all have our part to play. Without one of us, it wouldn't be Gracefall.

DB: It really comes across on the record.

JG: We're really proud of Surrender.

DB: Who inspired you to play the drums?

JG: Metallica, the Black Album. *I was thirteen at the time. My mother's boyfriend had left the CD at the house. I listened to that fucking thing a million times. I knew right away I wanted to play heavy and loud. The next thing I knew, I was looking through* DrumBeat, *searching the classifieds for drum lessons. That's where I found an ad from Leo Sterling, the God of Thunder. He brought out the best in my playing and as a person.*

There was a pause. He felt her eyes on him. "Dad would be flattered."

"It's the truth."

She continued.

DB: What advice would you have for someone wanting to follow in your footsteps?

JG: March to the beat of your own drum. Don't be afraid to go after your dreams. Play the loudest. Find one person at a show that isn't having a good time and rock their balls off.

DB: What is the most trouble you've ever gotten into?

Joe pulled into the parking lot and parked. "Are you done?" He tried again to snag the magazine but was unsuccessful.

"No way!" She hugged the embarrassing pages. "I'm getting to the good stuff."

JG: Oh, man. (He rubs the back of his neck.) Women. I love everything about them, which gets me in trouble from time to time. I'm a lover, not a fighter, but if someone comes talking smack, I can hold my own.

"Note to self, Joe Grace loves women," she laughed.

"Seriously, Mel, give me the damn thing."

She continued.

DB: Tits or ass man?

She cocked a brow, studying him for a brief second, which felt like an eternity. He didn't want her reading this part. "I think I know."

JG: Tits.

DB: Hell yeah! (I flashed my own pair of metal horns.)

"Tits, huh?"

Joe grabbed the magazine. "Okay, that's enough." He shoved it in the glovebox.

"I was thinking ass man," she joked.

"Drop it. It's only an interview. Means nothing." Joe jumped out of the Jeep and strode to the back of the car. He opened the hatch, gathering their bags. For fuck's sake, he should've burned the magazine. Mel would never let him live this one down.

Joe reached into the cargo space and grabbed a duffle bag. "Hey." He froze as her hand touched his arm. "It was a great interview. You have so much passion for what you do. And the critics love the new album. I'm proud of you."

Hearing those words coming from Mel made his heart swell. He'd made her proud. Joe straightened and locked his gaze on hers. "Really?"

"Really." She took the duffle from his hand. "I've listened to the album. It's amazing. I can't wait to see Gracefall live."

He treaded with suspicion, waiting for the joke. There was a joke coming.

"What?" She cocked her head to the side.

"I'm waiting for the joke." He shut the back of the Jeep.

"I'm not joking."

He picked up his duffle and one of Mel's, tossing them over his shoulder. "Your smile tells me differently."

They walked toward the bus side by side.

"Rock stars." She shook her head. "That's why I don't date them."

The confession should have ripped his heart out. Instead, it sparked a challenge. By the end of the tour, she'd change her mind.

He flung the duffle to the other shoulder, then put his arm around her. "Good thing I'm not a rock star."

7

The cold air rushed over Melody as she stepped up onto the bus. The new bus smell was refreshing, all new leather and natural wood scents. Not all buses smelled this good. By the end of the tour, it would be a different story.

"So, this is our home for the summer." Joe walked ahead, checking things out. "Oh, this is nice." He pointed to the bump-out. "This will give us some extra room."

Black leather couches lined the wall. She sat down and sank into the softness. "This is really nice." She brushed her hand across the leather. "Tour busses have come a long way since I've been on one."

Melody watched as Joe's smoldering gaze roamed over her crossed legs. Heat raced down her body and settled at her core. The friendship line was evaporating—quickly. Sharing close quarters with Joe Grace wasn't going to be easy.

"Let's take a look around." He offered her his hand.

"Sure." Anything to keep her mind off Joe.

She followed him into the kitchen. Neutral colors on the walls, cabinets, and countertops brighten the small area.

"Dylan is going to love this full kitchen." Joe opened the microwave. "Be prepared. He loves to cook."

"That's a plus." She opened an overhead cupboard. "Chips and more chips."

"Hell yeah." He continued leading her to the back of the bus. "Here's the bunks."

She pulled back the blackout bunk curtain. "TV and personal air conditioner—nice."

"Yeah, double bunks are nice." He leaned against it, patting the bed, and wiggled his brows. "Which one are you picking?"

She inspected the sleeping quarters. "Top."

"Note to self, Melody Sterling likes it on top."

"Touché." She laughed.

"I'll take the bottom." He continued down to the back of the bus, stopping at the end bunks. "These two are junk bunks. You can keep your bags in there." He grabbed her bags and stuffed them in.

Beneath his black Metallica tee, muscled, tattooed arms worked the bags to fit in the small space. By the looks of his well-defined body, he'd been hitting the gym regularly. Her eyes roamed down his broad back to his tight-fitting jeans. Until now, she'd never paid much attention to Joe's ass. Round, firm...he might be a tits man, but she was thoroughly enjoying being an ass girl. Wait, what was she thinking? This was Joe, her best friend. She needed to squash these sexual thoughts and feelings quick. She didn't date musicians, and she was definitely not falling for her best friend.

Note to self. Get it together.

Joe drew the curtain back, then turned to her. His smoldering eyes drew her in and held her captive. She couldn't look away if she wanted to. They stood, taking each other in.

She cleared her throat, breaking the spell. "So, when does the rest of the band show up?"

He looked at his watch. "Any time now." He leisurely sat on the black leather sectional couch that filled the back of the bus. His legs were spread wide, his arm resting on the back of the couch, a TV remote in hand. "You should check this out. Forty inches."

"Forty inches?" And here she thought his ass was impressive.

"Yep, forty-inch flat screen. Sweet!" He was like a kid in a candy shop.

She shook her head.

The door to the bus opened. "Hi, honey, I'm home!"

Melody's eyes widened, excited to hear Moxley's voice. "Moxie!" She rushed to the front of the bus.

"Oh, hell yeah!" Mox dropped his bags in time to catch her.

She hugged him tight, not realizing how much she'd missed him. Mox was the coolest dude she'd ever met. "I haven't seen you in forever. How's your wife?"

He placed her on her feet. "It's good to see you, Mellie Girl. When I told Sam you were joining us on tour, she squealed so loud over the phone my ears are still ringing."

She laughed. "I can't wait to see her."

"She'll join us in New York unless she has the baby before then."

"I bet you wish you could be home with her."

"Nah, she's a tough girl." He bumped shoulders with Joe as he greeted him. "Her sister is staying with her."

The bus door swung open again. Tyler stood in the doorway and belted out his best eighties metal scream, as if he were on stage. "Hey, motherfuckahs!" His face whitened as he saw her. "Oh shit, sorry about the language."

"I'll let it slide," she joked as she gave him a hug. "No need to change because I'm here."

"Uh, Mel," Joe said. "You might not want to give him that kind of freedom."

"And why's that?"

"Tyler's favorite food is Mexican."

"So?" She shrugged.

"Farts, Mel," Moxley shouted from the bunks. "The dude can light the place up."

"It's not that bad," Tyler argued, punching Mox's arm.

Melody shook her head. She was surrounded by men-children. Women, booze, tight living areas, and now farts. How in the hell was she going to survive the next four months? Not to mention her newly found attraction to Joe. She was in deep.

Outside, a car screeched to a halt. She knew who belonged to those squeaky breaks. Dani!

She looked out the window to confirm. A red two-door sports car was parked next to Joe's Jeep, Dani and Dylan inside.

"I'll be right back," she told Joe, then hurried outside. She had a few words to get off her chest.

She strode past Dylan, who had his arms held wide, waiting for her to hug him. "Oh fine, leave me hanging." He stood in his black leather jacket, shirtless, in feigned shock that she'd passed him by.

Melody looked over her shoulder and shrugged. She'd deal with Dylan later.

Knocking on the driver's side window, she motioned for Dani to roll it down.

Slowly the window lowered, and Dani smiled. "Hi."

"Don't 'hi' me." Melody stood with her hands on her hips. "I want the video deleted...right now."

"Don't be mad. You know you're thanking me right now. What woman wouldn't want to be on Gracefall's tour bus?" She sighed.

Melody rolled her eyes.

"Listen, this is the perfect time for you and Joe—"

"We're friends. That's it."

"Fine. You're friends. Put everything else aside. Take this time for yourself. You deserve some time away. Go tour the world."

Dani's gaze settled on Dylan as he made his way on the bus. Hurt burned in her friend's eyes. The situation between the two of them was toxic. It was an addictive, vicious cycle every time Dylan was in town. They'd hook up, and the next morning he'd leave, crushing Dani's hope that this time would be different—that he'd want more than a booty call. However long the dance went on, she'd be a wreck for weeks, pretending nothing was wrong—accepting friends with benefits.

Melody had always been there to help Dani pick up the pieces. "Hey, are you okay?"

On the outside, Dani looked as if she had it all together, but inside Melody knew she was an emotional mess.

"Look, I don't have to go. You need me. Joe will understand."

"No way. You're not getting out of this. Go. Have fun. And for the love of God, be naughty." A wicked grin spread across Dani's lips.

She leaned inside the little red sports car and hugged Dani. "You know I love you."

"I know."

The bus revved to life, ready to hit the road.

"You better go," Dani said. "Call me later."

"I will." She watched her friend leave the parking lot. Despair knotted in her stomach. This was why she didn't date rock stars. They're good fun to be around but were dangerous to your heart. There's only room for one woman in their lives, and she's *music*. She'd seen what rock and roll had done to her mother, and now Dani. But it was not going to happen to her.

~

*J*oe watched Mel through the window from the inside of the bus. His attention was drawn to her ass in those tattered, cutoff jean shorts.

Dylan stood next to him, pulling the curtain back. "Love is in the air," he sang.

"Shut the fuck up. We're just friends. You should know that." He continued to stare at Mel.

"It's never been just friends with Mel." Dylan ran his hand through his blond, crew-cut hair. "What were you thinking asking her on tour?"

He glared at Dylan. Obviously, he had something on his mind. "What do you mean?"

"We've never had a girl on the bus, touring with us. It changes the dynamics of things. Think about all the chicks you're giving up."

"I'm not giving up anything." He shrugged. "If I want to fuck, I'll fuck whoever I want."

"Delusional much?" Dylan snarked.

"Not at all. I know where I stand with Mel. We're permanently friend-zoned." He said it to save face with Dylan, but he knew they wouldn't be in the friend zone for long.

"So, you have no problem with Mel hooking up with

someone on tour? Or better yet, would you want her to see you with another woman? I don't think either one of you can handle it."

"You don't know shit."

"All I'm saying is if you want her, claim her before someone else does." Dylan pointed out the window at Mel. "Look, bro. She's gorgeous. And she likes your dumb ass."

Joe watched Mel as she walked toward the bus, mesmerized by the sway of her hips, the way she flipped her long blonde hair over her shoulder. He was crazy for her.

Somewhere in Dylan's brotherly lecture, he had a point. Mel couldn't be the one who got away.

"Hey, guys." Mel shut the door behind her. "Sorry about leaving you hanging, Dylan." She hugged him.

"Now, that's more like it." He smirked at Joe over Mel's shoulder.

"Looks like we're all here," Sal, the bus driver, said in his raspy, I need another cigarette voice. "Next stop, Idaho." He positioned himself behind the wheel, getting comfortable for the next fifteen hours.

Tyler strode to the front of the bus, holding two DVDs. "Slasher or monsters?"

Dylan grabbed a case. "Dude, *Friday the 13th*. Jason has my vote."

"Mr. Voorhees has my vote," Moxley called from the back of the bus as he played his guitar."

"The original or reboot?" Joe asked.

"The original." Dylan handed the movie case to Joe. "I'll make popcorn."

"Sweet!" He turned to Mel. "You up for a good horror flick?"

"I'll pass."

Like a needle scratching across a record, all eyes were on

Mel. Even Mox stopped playing and gazed down the bus at her.

"Um...I...should probably go over the itinerary." She peered up at Joe. "Why is everyone looking at me like I've grown two heads?"

"We have a superstition on the bus." Joe rubbed the back of his neck. "The beginning of every tour, we watch horror films. It's kinda bad luck if you don't watch."

"Oh." It was cute the way she wound a piece of her hair around her finger nervously.

"What's wrong?" He playfully poked her shoulder. "Scared?"

She tipped her chin. "I'm not scared of some make-believe character."

"Uh huh." He wrapped his arm around her shoulders and led her to the back of the bus.

Several hours and three movies later, the five of them lazed around the semi-circular black leather couch finally watching *Friday the 13th* on the big screen. After each horror flick, Mel's death grip tightened around Joe's arm, holding onto it for dear life. She'd moved closer until she was practically sitting on his lap, and he loved it.

No matter how hard he tried to keep his mind on the movie, he couldn't. Not with Mel's breasts pressed against his arm. If they were alone, he'd make a move, a bold one. He'd nuzzle her neck, kiss her hot flesh. He wouldn't think twice about crossing the line and slipping his hand up her shirt. His dick went hard, imagining the sweet sound of her moaning his name, begging for more.

Fuck yeah, he'd give it to her good.

He shifted in his seat, easing the tightness in his jeans.

"Oh my god." She gripped his arm. "Tell me the old man gets away."

"Wait for it." Dylan held up his hand. "Listen for the *ch ch ch, ah ah ah.*"

Silence sliced through the air as they sat on the edge of their seats, waiting for the kill.

The bus erupted in oohs and hell-yeahs as the old man fell victim to Jason Voorhees. Except for Mel. She buried her head against Joe's neck, holding onto him for dear life. "Tell me the old man's safe."

"What?" He snapped his head toward her. "You watched it, right?"

She shook her head. "Is it over?"

The guys busted into laughter.

Joe collected himself. "You seriously can't be afraid of Jason."

"Yeah, Mel." Moxley, who sat on the other side of her, rubbed her shoulder. "It's only a movie." He snorted.

"I can replay the scene," Dylan joked as he pointed the remote at the TV.

"No!" Mel sat up. "I'll pass."

"If you think about it, why would an old man be out in the woods sneaking a peek at the campers?" Joe tried to calm her down.

"To get his rocks off." Tyler made his best impression of a creepy peeper jerking off in the woods. Dylan joined in and added, "*ch ch ch, ah ah ah.*"

"Okay!" Mel stood. "On that note, I'm going to my bunk." She turned to the guys. "To SLEEP."

"Oh, come on." Joe grabbed her arm. "Stay. We'll behave."

"No, I've had enough of murder for one night. But y'all enjoy." She gave him a playful smile, then headed to the bunks.

"Sweet nightmares, Mellie," Dylan mocked. "Don't let the monsters bite."

Mel teasingly flipped him the bird.

"You're an asshole." Joe threw a throw pillow at his little bro.

Dylan caught the flying square of fluff before it reached his face. "What? I kid."

Joe shook his head. He wanted to go to Mel and make sure she was all right, but he couldn't, not in front of his bandmates. They'd notice his attraction toward her and never let him live it down. For now, he had to keep things on the downlow.

He waited a few minutes for Mel to settle into her bunk before he whipped out his cellphone and texted her.

Joe: Sorry. You all right?

Not wanting to draw attention to himself, he put the phone down and waited for her text. A minute later, it vibrated.

Melody: I'm fine.

Joe: Are you sure? I could come and tuck you in.

He prayed he hadn't crossed the line.

Melody: And read me a bedtime story?

He heard the sarcasm in her tone.

Joe: Not sure if I can find a book on the bus. However, I'm sure Dylan has a Playboy *lying around. I hear their articles are highly informative.*

Melody: Oh, I love picture books...not! Goodnight, Joe.

Disappointment didn't even describe what he was feeling. He'd hoped she'd accept his offer. Not about the *Playboy*, necessarily, but he could find a hundred other ways to soothe her nerves. However, he had her for the next four months. He had plenty of time to change her mind.

Joe: Sweet dreams, Mel.

8

*M*elody woke up to the sound of Moxley strumming his guitar and the smell of bacon. She rolled over, and to her surprise she wasn't woozy—the bus wasn't moving. All night she'd fought waves of nausea, praying she'd keep the contents of her stomach down. The constant rocking and rolling of the bus had given her a bad case of motion sickness. Yep, it had been a while since she'd been on a bus.

She grabbed her phone and checked the time. *Ten o'clock.* Shit, she'd overslept. The bus had arrived in Idaho right on time, which meant she was two hours behind.

Melody slipped out of the bunk, still feeling unsteady on her feet. She hoped this would pass, or else she was going to be miserable the rest of the tour. First thing on her to-do list, find some Dramamine.

She wobbled her way to the back of the bus to find her suitcase in the junk bunk. She fumbled through it, finding a casual black mini dress, a jean jacket, and her cosmetic tote. On her way to the bathroom, she passed Joe's bunk. The curtain had been pulled back, and he was gone. Her guess, breakfast. Where there was bacon, there was Joe.

The bathroom was no more than an upscale version of a Porta Potty with a shower. Not that Melody was complaining. She'd seen worse. Sharing this bathroom with four guys, she touched as little as possible. Deciding to skip a shower, she went straight for the dry shampoo and baby wipes. As she brushed through her hair, pulling it back into a ponytail, her mind was on Joe...still on Joe. Last night, she couldn't shake the thought of him tucking her into bed—lying next to her... kissing...touching. She shook her head, erasing the fantasy.

Instead of being with Joe, she'd spent the night nauseous and looking over the itinerary. Sexually satisfying...not at all.

What was wrong with her? The more she was around him, the more she wanted him, and that couldn't happen.

Melody took a long look in the mirror as she applied lip gloss. She had a job to do. She needed to post the band's schedule. Interviews, sound checks, the list went on. She had to check on the roadies and make sure there weren't any problems setting up the equipment. She had to give the food supply team the band's menu. She didn't know if there were enough hours in the day to get everything done.

Melody collected her things and opened the door. As she stepped out, she froze. Dylan stood in the kitchen, cooking in the buff.

"Oh my god!" She looked away. "I did not need to see that."

"My bad!" He rummaged through a drawer, pulling out an apron. "I should have warned you. I cook naked."

Melody put her tote back in the junk bunk, then made her way to the kitchen. "Thanks for the warning, but the damage is done," she teased as she scooted past him to the small kitchen table where her laptop was plugged in.

"You are in the presence of greatness." Dylan placed a plate of food in front of her. He stood as if he was on display, motioning to his body. "I'm a golden god, baby."

She rolled her eyes. His ego was larger than life—that hadn't changed. His confidence had no limits, which was why he was Gracefall's front man. Ladies loved him. Men wanted to be him.

Melody took a bite of the omelet. *Oh. My. God.* He also knew how to cook. "This is delicious." She took another bite.

Dylan stood, watching her eat, proud of himself. "Not only is it tasty, it's healthy. Egg whites, spinach, and mush-rooms. Turkey bacon on the side."

"I'm impressed." Dylan was hot all right, almost as hot as his brother. And he cooked. Now she understood why Dani allowed the booty calls. She got gourmet omelets.

"Dylan has had a lot of practice." Moxley joined her at the table. "He cooks breakfast for all of his ladies."

"Hey, the least I can do is thank them with a hot breakfast." Dylan went back to the small stovetop, tending to another omelet. The apron fell short to cover him, and his ass hung out.

She focused on the plate in front of her as she giggled. She'd seen enough of his ass for the day, no, for the rest of her life.

This was life on the bus, and it had just started. As she ate, she opened her laptop, pulled up the itinerary, and printed out a schedule.

The bus door swung open, and in walked Joe. Her eyes went straight to his shirtless, sweaty chest. He'd been out for a run.

He removed his earbuds. "Hey, I stopped by and snagged a couple concert tees." He tossed one to Dylan and Moxley, then handed one to her.

At least she'd thought he had. She couldn't tear her eyes away from the sweat winding its way down his chest and into the waistband of his shorts.

Joe sat next to her. Heat radiated off his body like an inferno. "So, what's on the schedule, boss?" He leaned over, peeking at her laptop.

He was way too close for her liking.

She cleared her throat. "Soundcheck at five, meet and greet at six." His arm rubbed against hers, and she lost all concentration. "Um...I printed out a schedule. I can go get it."

"No worries." He smiled, and she melted.

"I'm telling you," Moxley said with a mouth full of food. "If I weren't married, I'd make Dylan my bitch. This omelet is delicious."

Melody was grateful for the interruption. Her mind had taken a naughty trip down Joe Highway. She needed to pull over and get off, because avoiding the attraction always worked...not.

Joe leaned back. "And here I thought you'd marry Dylan for the way his ass looked in an apron."

They turned an eye to Dylan. He smacked his bare ass. "You know it, baby."

Melody laughed. "Yeah, I got the full monty picture this morning."

"What?" Joe sat up and turned to her. "You saw Dylan naked?"

"Who hasn't?" Moxley shoved another fork full of fluffy eggs into his mouth.

"Hey." Dylan pointed the spatula at them. "If you got it, flaunt it."

Tyler shuffled in from the bunks, bedhead and all. "What's for breakfast, Sweet Cheeks?" He smacked Dylan on the ass on the way to the table.

"See," Dylan threw his hands in the air. "Someone who appreciates a nice ass."

"So," Melody interrupted the awkward moment, which obviously only affected her. To the guys, this was normal banter. "I have a schedule for everyone. I'll post one up in the kitchen and text one to your phones. Is there anyone here who needs extra reminders?" She grabbed her phone and sent everyone their schedules.

"Nope." Tyler yawned. "I'm good."

The rest of the guys nodded.

Joe leaned in again, invading her space. "What's your schedule like?"

God, even sweaty, he smelled good. "I'm swamped. I have to check in on the roadies, then hospitality, lighting, and sound managers, and I have a teleconference with management."

"So, you're available for lunch. I'll pick up something from the food tent."

"I'm not sure—"

"Great." He snagged a strip of bacon off her plate. "I'll see you later." He winked and left the table.

And just like that, she had one hell of a sexy lunch date.

∽

*T*he park across the street from the venue was a perfect spot to meet Joe for lunch. Melody waited for him on the park bench. No one was here, which didn't surprise her; it was summer, and it was hot.

"Hey." Joe jogged up to her, holding a white paper bag. "Sorry I'm late."

She scooted over, inviting him to sit. "That's okay. I just got here."

He sat down and opened the bag. "I have chicken sandwiches and brownies."

"Sounds great." She took the sandwich he offered and pulled back the bun. "You remembered, no tomatoes."

He shrugged, playing it cool.

Melody was starving, so she dug in. After the second mouthful, she felt his eyes on her and looked up. "What?"

He smiled and wiped the corner of her mouth. "Feels just like old times."

Mortified she'd been eating like a pig, she swallowed down the mouthful of chicken. "Yeah, it's nice. I just can't figure out when you became so sexy."

"You think I'm sexy."

"Look at you." She rubbed his bicep. "I don't remember these."

"Working out keeps me out of trouble." He winked and took a bite of his sandwich.

By the look of his body, he'd spent every free minute in the gym.

"You look good, too, Melody." He looked her up and down. "Then again, you've always been beautiful."

Shyly, she tucked a strand of hair behind her ear. Why did she feel so awkward?

"Remember the summer of '09 when your father took us

on tour with him?" He changed the subject.

Of course, she did. It had been the best time of her life. She was thirteen, and he was fifteen. They'd snuck off to watch the opening acts on tour with her father's legendary band, Twofold. They raised hell in the front row with their fists to the sky. Adrenaline pumped through their veins like a drug. Music was their addiction. "I do."

"Good times." He nodded.

"The best." She'd had fond memories hanging out with Joe. His charm drew her in. He didn't care that her father was a rock and roll god. He treated her like a normal person when everyone else around her only liked her for who her father was.

"Except that time at the Metallica concert when I almost got my ass kicked. Remember?"

She laughed. "I do."

How could she not remember? A guy at the concert who had been standing behind her had his hands on her butt. It was the first time she'd heard Joe announce her ass was his, and if the dude had a problem with it, he'd fix it.

"You laugh now, but the dude had his hands all over your ass."

"Good times." She laughed.

"I couldn't image raising hell with anyone else but you." His hand brushed over hers, and her heart raced. She saw it in his eyes. He wanted her as much she wanted him.

Her eyes fell to his lips, and a rush of heat came over body. All she had to do was lean forward and finally know how it would feel to be kissed by Joe Grace, the rock star.

"Well, that's what friends are for." She pulled her hand away, breaking free from the temptation.

He leaned back on the bench and exhaled. "Friends."

She felt his disappointment, too, but she wasn't ready to

cross the line. If she lost Joe's friendship...she didn't want to think about it.

"Hey, I almost forgot." She watched Joe pull out an outdated iPod from his pocket. "I filled it with songs we used to listen to under the live oak tree at your house when we were kids."

"Are you serious?" She took the device. "This looks like the same iPod. Where did you find it?"

"You can find anything on the internet if you look hard enough."

She laughed. "What songs did you download?"

"You'll have to listen to it." He flashed her a wicked smile.

She hugged him. "Thank you. I can't wait to listen."

"Sometimes a song says everything you can't." He held her hand. "Listen carefully, Melody." His steel-gray stare sent a shiver down her spine. This was more than a thoughtful gift. *What message was he trying to send?*

"I will." Her throat went dry as her eyes settled once again on his lips. She looked away, avoiding another intimate moment. "But right now, we should get back. Soundcheck is in an hour."

"Whatever you say, Boss Lady. Are you coming to the show tonight?"

"Absolutely," she beamed. It had been over a year since she'd seen the guys play. She couldn't wait to hear their new material live.

"Rock on." He gave her a wicked smile. Heat shot up her body. His advances were relentless. Little by little, he was wearing her resolve down. And then what? How was she going to survive Joe Grace?

෴

*M*elody stood on floor level, center of the arena, barricaded behind a digital soundboard with Gracefall's sound engineer, Jimmy. Whiplash had finished, the lights were back on, and the fans were lining up at the concession stands. She'd introduced herself, asked a few questions, and made sure Jimmy was on top of things. He was, which made her job a lot easier. She grabbed a seat out of Jimmy's way and allowed him to do his job.

With time to spare, Melody reached inside her bag and pulled out the iPod Joe had given her. She unwrapped the headphone cord from around the device, then put the buds in her ears. She was surprised she remembered how to turn it on. She scrolled through the menu and highlighted music.

An image of Shinedown appeared with their song, "If You Only Knew."

Melody's heart skipped a beat. She remembered the song well. She closed her eyes, listening to the lyrics and remembering them lying under the live oak. Many times, she'd wished for Joe to kiss her.

The song ended and "Beast of Burden" followed. A huge smile spread across her face. *Prom.*

As she put the songs together and remembered Joe telling her to listen carefully, she began to see his message. She didn't know if she could listen anymore. If her gut was right, it was telling her that Joe had always been in love with her.

It couldn't be. She scanned through the songs, and right there after the fifth song, she believed it. Joe had wanted to be more than just friends. She placed her hand over her mouth to hide her huge smile. Was this a good thing? Of course not.

Her phone vibrated, interrupting her thoughts. She slid open her phone. Her heart skipped a beat when she saw a text from Joe.

Joe: Are you listening?

God, how was she supposed to answer that?

Melody: I am.

Joe: What song are you on?

Melody: If You Only Knew.

Joe: Now you know.

Melody: I think I do. We should talk about this.

Joe: In time. Where are you?

Melody: I'm here with Jimmy. I've got an amazing floor seat.

Joe: Rock on! Have I told you lately I'm glad you're here with me?

Melody: Not since lunch.

She added a wink emoji.

Joe: Ha, funny. I can't wait to see you after the show.

He sent a selfie with him and Mox backstage, devil horns up and a Dylan photo bomb. She laughed. The excitement in the picture was contagious. She wished she were backstage with him.

Melody: I'll see ya after the show.

Joe: Gotta go. Wish me luck.

Melody: You don't need luck. Go rock everyone's balls off!

Joe: Lol

The lights went down, and the crowd of 50,000 chanted, "Gracefall...Gracefall!" The excitement grew as the band took the stage. Melody flew to her feet, screaming and cheering, feeling like the thirteen-year-old girl from that summer.

Mox and Tyler took the stage first, adjusting their guitars. She screamed louder as Joe walked on stage in his black, tight Metallica t-shirt with the sleeves cut out. He pumped his fists to the fans before he sat behind his drum kit. The bass drum thundered through the arena and straight to her heart.

The crowd exploded, pushing the needle to the red zone, as Dylan stood center stage in his white, ribbed tank and black dress pants.

"Idaho!" Dylan screamed. He held up devil horns and stuck out his pierced tongue. "What's up, motherfuckahs!"

The crowd went wild, electric.

"We're Gracefall," he growled into the mic, his voice vibrating through every single person's spine.

Power chord.

Deep bass.

Rock-solid beats.

Growling vocals.

The arena went electric, like a switch had been turned on. The crowd sang along, headbanging with their fists in the air as Dylan hit them brutally with emotionally charged lyrics. It amazed her how much Gracefall had impacted so many people. Their music came from the heart, there was nothing fake about it.

Melody fixed her sights on Joe. She saw a lot of her dad's influence on Joe's playing. Immaculate drumming, hard-hitting power play—her father would be proud of him.

Joe was the heartbeat of the song, the sexy beast behind the machine. The rock star she swore she'd never fall for.

9

*A*fter weeks on the road playing nonstop, Joe wanted some alone time with Mel. Flirting and sitting next to her on the bus wasn't cutting it. The iPod gift had cracked opened the door of possibilities, and it was time he made a move, preferably without having his bandmates as an audience.

Joe pulled his cell out and Googled things to do around...where the hell were they? North Carolina, Podunk somewhere.

Mox sat down next to him in the back of the bus. "Tyler found a bar about five miles up the road. You in?"

Not really. He didn't want to bring Mel to a bar. He wanted more privacy.

"I'm in," Dylan said from his bunk. "What kind of bar is it?" He hopped down.

"It's called Toot's Honky-tonk," Mox answered in his best country twang.

"Sweet!" Dylan exclaimed. "I have a pair of assless chaps I've been dying to wear."

Mel, who was sitting at the corner table on her laptop, busted into laughter. "Are you serious?"

"Damn straight," Dylan smirked.

"As your tour manager, I strongly suggest you reconsider your bar attire." Mel glanced over at Joe. "You're not going to allow him off the bus with assless chaps on, are you?"

Joe shrugged. "He's a big boy."

"Mel, you're in, right?" Mox asked.

"I'm sure she doesn't want to hang out at a bar," Joe said. "I'll stay here."

He hoped he wasn't too transparent about his intentions. With the guys at the bar, he and Mel would have the bus to themselves. Not very romantic, but at least they would be alone.

"No, I'll go," Mel said. "Someone needs to hold your bail money."

The vision Joe had of making out with Mel on the couch burned to ashes. There was no escaping these guys.

"Well." He rubbed his hands down his jean-clad thighs. "Looks like we're going to Toot's."

An hour later, they were piling into Joe's drum tech's Toyota Camry. Joe decided to drive. He'd be the only one sober enough to drive back to the bus. Mox was sitting in the back between Dylan and Tyler, giving Joe directions to Toot's. Mel was sitting next to him in her ass-hugging jeans and a tight red tank top. She looked beautiful with her long, wavy blonde hair hanging over her shoulders. Hell, she'd look beautiful wearing a garbage bag. He glanced at her, and she smiled, lip gloss shimmering on her lips. Damn. He fought the urge to pull over and kiss her speechless.

"Turn right at the next light," Mox said, bringing his attention back on the road.

Joe made the next right, then pulled into the gravel

parking lot. Toot's flashed in white lights in front of the bar. Wasting no time, Tyler, Mox, and Dylan piled out of the car. Joe and Mel followed. As they entered the bar, they stuck out like a sore thumb with their long hair and rock tees, but Joe didn't care, as long as no one noticed they were Gracefall.

As Tyler, Mox, and Dylan found their way to the bar, Joe and Mel grabbed a table. A country music band played on stage, and a sea of cowboy hats and Wrangler jeans line danced to the music. This was so not his scene.

A bleach-blonde waitress in short shorts and a Toot's crop top stopped over. "What ya havin', Darlin'?" She smiled at Joe as if she wanted to eat him alive.

"I'll have a beer. Whatever's on tap." He winked, then looked at Mel.

"And what can I get the lucky lady?" Bleach Blondie turned her attention to Mel.

Mel kept her eyes on Joe. "I'll have what he's having." She handed the menu back without looking at Blondie.

Once the waitress left, Mel raised a brow. "She totally wants you."

"I don't know what you're talkin' about, Darlin'," he replied in a twang.

"Right." She tucked her hair behind her ear. Damn, she was sexy. "Blondie was flirting with you. I bet by the end of the night she'll be giving you her number."

Joe leaned in. "What are we betting? I know what I want." He smirked.

She bit her bottom lip as she thought about a wager. "If I win and she gives you her number, you have to dance with me on the dance floor for one song of my choosing."

He eyed her as he stroked his beard and thought of a wager. He couldn't tell her he wanted to kiss her senseless, not yet. Besides, that was happening tonight. His gaze traveled to the black lace bra sticking out from the top of her low-cut tank top. "If I win," he smiled. "I want to see you dance on top of the bar."

"Oh, you think you're funny, Rock Star?"

"No. I just want to see you dance again." He winked.

"Fine." She offered her hand. "You got a deal. Get your dancing shoes on, because you're going down."

He shook her hand and smiled. "We'll see."

"See what?" With a drink in hand, Mox sat down next to Mel.

"We made a bet. See that blonde waitress over there?" Mel tipped her chin toward Blondie.

"The one with her ass cheeks hanging out of her short shorts?" Mox took a long drink.

Mel rolled her eyes. "Yes. She took our drink order and was practically eye-fucking Joe."

"Well, he is a sexy beast," Mox agreed and smiled at Joe.

"We have a bet going. I say by the end of the night, she gives Joe her number. If she does, and we all know she will, Joe has to dance with me." Mel leaned back in her chair and crossed her arms over her chest, smirking in victory at Joe.

"And if you lose?" Mox asked.

"Mel has to dance on the bar," Joe said.

Mox looked at Mel. "I'm sorry, sweetie, but I'm with Joe on this one."

She shook her head. "You both are dirty dogs."

Joe and Mox shrugged at each other, accepting the fact they were dogs.

Ten minutes later Blondie returned with two frosty mugs. She gave Mel hers first, then turned her attention to Mox. Before she could say a word, he flashed her his wedding ring. She sat the second mug down in front of Joe, then slipped him a note. "I get off at midnight." She glanced at Mel. "Bring your girlfriend, too." She winked at her before sauntering off.

"Oh, shit," Mox laughed into his fist.

"Well, what do you say, honey?" Joe wiggled his brows at her. "Welcome to my world."

"Wow." Mel's mouth fell open. "I did not see that coming." She tipped the mug back and took a long sip of beer.

"Me neither." Joe opened the note and tossed it on the table. "Looks like I owe you a dance."

She picked up the piece of paper and read the digits. "You know I'm not the type of person who says told you so, but—"

"Don't say it." Joe put his hands up.

Even though he was a drummer and could hold down a beat, dancing wasn't his thing, but he'd do it for her. They'd finally be alone.

The house band returned to the stage. They were decent for a local band. Joe remembered those early days of playing in bars. They'd play any place, as long there was a crowd, and Gracefall had always packed a house. It was a time when the band formed a tight brotherly bond. When they were on stage, the four of them were one unit, playing off one another, playing music they loved.

He looked across the table at Mel. She was the only one he wanted to share this experience with. Could he have a successful band and the woman he loved? Hell yeah, he could.

The sexual, soulful beat of "Beast of Burden" began to play, and he knew what was coming next. This was her favorite song. It was their song.

She gave him a knowing smile.

He stood and offered her his hand, then nodded to the dance floor. If he had to dance, he was going all in. He'd hold nothing back. By the end of the night, she'd know exactly what he wanted.

The dance floor was crowded, but he found an empty spot. They stood facing each other, waiting for the other to make the first move. It was like they both knew they were crossing the friendship line. He didn't wait long; he wrapped her arms around his neck. Slowly, he trailed his hands down her arms, her sides, to her hips. He held her against his body and rested his forehead against hers. Their hips swayed with the beat as he sang to her.

Shivers raced down his spine as her fingers lightly caressed the back of his shaven head. Lost in her touch, he couldn't focus on the lyrics. He wanted her hands all over him. Hell, he wanted his hands all over her.

He slid his hands across her hips to her ass. The soft globes felt fucking amazing in the palms of his hands. His dick went hard, and his inner barbarian surfaced, urging him to throw her over his shoulder, find a dark corner, and make out.

As if she'd read his mind, her nipples hardened against his chest. The heavy look in her eyes told him she wanted him as much as he wanted her, if that was even possible.

He caressed her cheek, gazing deep into her hazel eyes, remembering the last time they had danced. It was at her senior prom, and it was the first time he'd realized he wanted more than just friendship. All night he'd thought of ways to steal a kiss, but in the end, he'd walked her to her door and awkwardly gave her a hug, then left.

Now, it felt right.

He slipped a hand behind her neck and dipped his head

down. He could feel her sweet breath on his lips when someone yelled out, "Fight!"

The music suddenly stopped, and the opportunity was lost. The crowd on the dance floor made a mad dash toward the bar. Being taller than most, Joe saw the commotion. "Fuck!"

Dylan had a husky, cowboy hat-wearing dude in a head-lock. Beer bottles were flying. Fists were flying. Joe had to break this up before Dylan ended up in jail.

"Go to the car!" he shouted to Mel.

"Want's going on?" She stood on her tiptoes, trying to find out.

"Dylan!"

A man in Wrangler jeans and a black Stetson bumped into her, pushing her into Joe. He caught her. "What the fuck!" he yelled and shoved the man.

"You want some of this?" Mr. Stetson puffed out his chest and approached him. The dude was short, and had the Napoleon Complex down to a T.

Joe wasn't looking for a fight. However, Napoleon had shoved his girl. Besides, just the sight of him pissed Joe off. He cocked back his fist and punched him in the face, sending him flat on his ass.

"Joe!" Mel shouted, looking at him in shock. "What the hell?"

"You need to get out of here. Go to the car and wait for me."

She shook her head, then headed to the nearest exit.

Thirty minutes later, Joe and the guys were outside under the lighted Toot's sign, giving their statements to the cops.

Mel walked over to Joe with her arms crossed. "So, who are we bailing out tonight?"

"Dylan better pray the officer hauls his ass to jail. Asshole." He paced in front of her, rubbing the tension from the back of his neck. "He's always screwing around where he shouldn't. He's going to fuck things up."

"I'm sure there's a reasonable explanation for the fight."

"If you call Dylan hitting on another man's woman reasonable, then sure."

"Yeah, that's not going to go over too well."

"Hey!" Dylan walked toward them with the cop, holding a bloody towel wrapped in ice to his nose. The officer looked young. A rookie. "You'll never guess who our biggest fan is."

"Oh my god, Dylan," Mel exclaimed and rushed to examine his nose. "Is it broken?"

"No." The cop said. "The paramedic said to keep ice on it, and the swelling will go down."

"Bro, check this out." Dylan turned to his new friend. "Go ahead, show them."

The rookie rolled up his sleeve, proudly showing off a tattoo of Gracefall's logo. "I've been a fan from the beginning. I've seen at least ten of your shows."

"Holy shit!" Joe came closer, getting a better look at the tat. The flames surrounding the guitar were on point. "Guys, check this out." He motioned for Mox and Tyler to look.

"That's hardcore, bro," Tyler said as he held his ribs, obviously having been involved in a fight of his own. From the statement he'd given, Tyler had tried to rescue Dylan and ended up thrown over the bar.

Fucking assholes! All he wanted was one night without one of his bandmates ending up in jail. That wasn't too much to ask, right?

Mox put out a cigarette on the bottom of his boot. "You should come to the show tomorrow night."

"I'm on duty." The cop handed Joe a piece a paper for his autograph.

"Sorry you'll miss the show," Joe said as he signed the paper, then gave it to Tyler.

"No worries. Tonight was better than a show. I can't believe I'm here with Gracefall. Hot damn!"

"So, are we good here, officer?" Mel asked.

The warmth from the officer's face disappeared. Joe knew it—someone was going to the pokey.

"The owner of the bar doesn't want to press charges. He saw the whole thing go down. As far as I'm concerned, Dylan was defending himself."

Joe sighed in relief.

"However."

Joe froze. This wasn't good.

"The owners don't want y'all to ever come back."

"Not a problem, officer." Joe shook his hand. "I promise no more trouble from us."

A few more autographs and handshakes later, they were heading toward the car. Dylan put his arm around Mel, staggering. "Y'all don't come back now, ya hear?" he mocked.

"Shut up, asshole." Joe smacked him upside the head. It took all his might not to kick his brother's ass. Not only did little bro cock block him, but he'd also punched a guy right in front of Mel. Dylan must look like an idiot to her.

They piled inside the car. Mel sat in the back with Dylan and Tyler. Mox called shotgun.

"Hey Mellie, Mel, Mellie," Dylan slurred. "I need some TLC."

Joe watched from the rearview mirror as Dylan laid his head down on her lap. "You need to leave her alone."

"I'm fine." She looked at Joe through the mirror and

winked. "Let's take a peek." She removed the ice. "It's still bleeding, but you'll live."

"Hey, Joe," Dylan slurred. "Do you remember mom telling me I'd live after her boyfriend put his cigar out on my chest? I was like...what...ten or something?"

"Dylan, you're drunk." Joe glanced in the rearview. Mel was shooting him a confused look. "You have no idea what you're saying." Joe prayed he'd dismissed the truth, but by the look in Mel's eyes, he'd have to explain that little trip down memory lane.

Dylan looked up at Mel. "You want to see the scar?"

"No," Mel said. "I think you should stop talking before I kick your ass. You are clueless. Do you realize how lucky you were tonight? You should have been arrested. And there's a show tomorrow. How was Gracefall supposed to perform with their singer behind bars?"

"You don't have to use your mommy voice. Damn." Dylan sat up.

"Obviously, I do. You're a freaking man-child."

Joe held in a laugh. Finally, someone had put Dylan in his place.

～

*J*oe stayed outside as Mox and Tyler took Dylan inside the bus. He was too angry to deal with Dylan's drunken stupidity. He knew exactly what Dylan had been talking about in the car, but he wouldn't acknowledge it. Not in front of Melody. No way in hell would he bring her into the darkness. His family, or lack of, was his secret. He'd never tell her about his mother being a drug addict. She'd never know about the multiple men coming in and out of their lives when they were kids.

She'd never know about the abuse. As far as she knew, his mother was a travel nurse, serving the sick. Hell, he even lived the lie.

As a kid, Joe had never set out looking for a fight. Being bigger than most kids his age, bullies had left him alone. However, Dylan was another story—he was skinny and an easy target. Joe had protected Dylan, except for that night. He'd been too late. His mom's boyfriend had beat the hell out of Dylan while he was over at Melody's house. When he'd got home and saw what had taken place, he'd pulled out the baseball bat from under his bed and attacked her boyfriend. To this day, he can still hear the crack as he hit the douchebag upside the head. He'd sent the asshole to the hospital.

The incident had been locked up and sealed. Not even the paparazzi could unearth that dirt. However, he'd always live with the guilt. Not for busting the douchebag's face—he deserved it. He'd failed his brother. He shouldn't have left him alone. Dylan had suffered, but for how long and to what extent, he didn't know. Little bro never talked about it.

Dylan was running with the devil, hiding his demons. It was only a matter of time before he spiraled out of control. How much longer could he ignore the ticking time bomb ready to explode?

"Hey." Mel stood beside him, leaning against the car. "You all right?"

"Yeah, I'm good." He glanced at her. The troubled look on her face broke his heart. She didn't deserve to be brought into his mess.

"Dylan's going to have one hell of a hangover in the morning. Better make some of your famous hangover concoction." She shivered.

"Right." He laughed, remembering the time he'd made it

for her. It had only been weeks ago, but right now it felt like a lifetime.

Silence fell over them as he thought of the right words to say. He didn't want the night to end like this. He wanted that kiss.

He looked at her hand, splayed on the car, and brushed his thumb over it. "I enjoyed dancing with you tonight."

She watched him trace small circles on her skin. "Me too. Reminds me of the time you took me to the senior prom." She smiled. "Every girl there had been jealous that I took bad boy Joe Grace to prom. You know, when you graduated, you left behind a bad reputation of breaking hearts."

He'd graduated two years before her. When she'd hinted she didn't have a date for prom, he'd flown home from a gig to take her.

"Nah, I remember it differently. Every girl wanted to be you, and every boy wanted to be with you."

She looked up. "Well, I guess there's two sides to every story."

"Yeah." He bumped her shoulder with his. "You know your father scared the crap out of me."

"What do you mean?"

"I never told you, but when I went to your father and asked him if I could take you to prom, he threatened to shoot me."

"Get out." She shoved his shoulder. "I don't believe you."

"He sure did. When I came over to ask, he was sitting behind his desk in the basement, cleaning his shotgun. When I finished asking, he cocked the gun and pointed it at me."

"You're serious?"

"Yep. He told me to keep my dick in my pants, or he'd use it for target practice."

"Oh my god!" She did a facepalm. "I always wondered why you didn't kiss me goodnight."

Joe paused. Did he hear her right? "You wanted me to kiss you?"

She hid her face in her hands and nodded.

He pulled her in front of him and placed his hands on her hips. Maybe he could make up for that night. "Can I kiss you now?"

She stepped into his embrace, wrapping her arms around his neck. "I thought you'd never ask."

She drew him in with the heavy look in her eyes as he slid his hand behind her neck, bringing her mouth to his. Her body shuddered as he kissed her softly, delicately, like butterfly wings sweeping across her lips. He breathed her in, cherry lip gloss and all.

Her touch set his body on fire, sending a buzz rushing in his veins, urging him to kiss her deeper. His tongue slipped past her lips, and her breathing quickened. The way she responded to his kiss rocked him to the core. It was like the world had stopped and his fantasy had come true. Fuck yeah, he was kissing Melody Sterling.

After tonight, things between them would never be the same again.

She broke the kiss, giving them both time to catch their breaths. He rested his forehead against hers. She felt like heaven in his arms, yet inside, he burned to feel her naked skin against his. His dick hardened, imagining her lying naked beneath him.

She licked her lips and closed her eyes. "What are we doing?"

Tucking her hair behind her ear, he caressed the side of her cheek. "Being us."

~

*M*elody lay in her bunk in a haze. In one passionate moment, Joe had rocked her to the core. Their friendship was on the line, yet kissing him felt right. Being here on tour with Joe felt right. Everything about Joe felt right. But it also felt wrong, like they had betrayed their pact. Would things between them turn awkward now? God, she hoped not.

Maybe it was just one kiss, and she was overthinking the situation.

Frustrated, she rolled over, gazing up at the gray, suede headliner. What was Joe thinking right now? Was he analyzing the kiss like she was? Probably not. Among many things she loved about Joe, she admired his ability to live in the moment. Not her. Right now, she was mentally collecting data for her pros and cons list.

They really needed to talk about this.

The bunk curtains flew back, causing her to jerk. "Hey, scoot over," Joe said as he climbed into her bunk.

Before she could move, he made himself comfortable. In her bunk! "What are you doing?" she whispered as she scooted until her back was against the wall.

"After that kiss, I'm not sleeping." The mattress gave as he shut the curtains and lay down. "Want to cuddle?"

Her eyes roamed down his naked chest, taking in his tattooed muscles. She swallowed past the lump in her throat. Good God, he was sexy. She was in trouble. No. No. No.

"I promise I'll be a good boy." He shot her a wicked smile, and she melted.

"I'm not worried about you, Rock Star." That was a lie. "It's the other guys in the band. Doesn't look professional for their tour manager to be cuddling with their drummer."

He shrugged. "Dylan's passed out, Tyler sleeps with earbuds on, and Mox, let's just say he's on an important phone call with Sam." He winked.

She eased down into the bed and hugged the sheet, creating a thin barrier between their bodies. The way he made her feel right now, she didn't trust herself.

"Why are you way over there?" he pulled her close. "Everything okay?"

No, everything wasn't okay. She was falling for her best friend, and it was freaking her out. "Maybe this isn't a good idea."

"What? Cuddling?"

"No. I mean, kinda, yeah. We promised each other to never cross that line, and here we are, dancing right across it. You know what sex, drugs, and rock and roll will do to a relationship."

"I know." He folded his hands on his chest. "It's scary, but, Mel, I can't hold back anymore." He looked at her. "I want more than your friendship. If you don't want the same, tell me now."

She did want more. Always had.

Her eyes roamed over his tattooed chest as she thought about what to say. The Celtic cross over his right pectoral, the same one she'd seen the morning he'd stood in her kitchen, caught her attention. Being closer now she could read the word in Celtic font inside the cross. Was that her name? In awe, she traced the letters lightly with her fingertip. "Melody?"

He held her hand and placed it on his heart. He gazed deeply into her eyes with the most honest expression she'd ever seen from Joe. "It's a reminder that our friendship is the cross I bear. I have loved you since the day I met you, but I valued our friendship, so I never told you."

"I don't know what to say."

"You don't have to say anything."

Words couldn't describe the love she felt right now. He'd laid it all on the line. Stripped bare for her to see his true feelings. She felt the same way.

She leaned over and placed a kiss inside the cross. The salty taste of his skin turned her on as she moved upward, kissing him tenderly up his chest to his neck. His arm tightened around her waist and pulled her close. "I love you, Joe Grace. Always," she whispered.

He exhaled heavily as if a boulder had been lifted from his chest. "You have no idea how good it feels to finally hear you say that."

"I think I do." She trailed her finger down his jawline, loving the way his steel-gray eyes were set on hers. "Promise me if things don't work out, we'll still be friends."

"I promise."

And she believed him with all her heart. Joe had never given her a reason not to trust him. She laid her head on his chest, taking in his fresh, sandalwood scent and relaxed into his arms. "Whatever is happening between us, I like being us."

He hugged her tight and kissed the top of her head. "Me too, Melody."

10

*T*he rhythmic humming of white noise filled the tour bus as Melody sat in the back at her window-seat desk, working, or at least pretending to. She couldn't keep her mind off Joe, who was sitting on the couch playing video games. They were finally alone, with the rest of the guys either sleeping or lounging in their bunks.

A week down and two more shows to go left little time with Joe. The quick kisses here and there weren't cutting it, not when she saw firsthand how the groupies dressed and acted backstage. They did anything to get noticed, which always started with flashing their tits as an ice breaker. She'd seen enough perfect cleavage that she started to feel insecure about her own. Boobs are so overrated.

Backstage, the party didn't stop. However, it did for her. She faded into the background while the groupies picked the boys apart like vultures. Joe loved his fans, though he didn't cross the line. Dylan and Tyler...they indulged, recently adding a threesome to their resume.

She needed to up her game. Cute and cuddly wasn't

cutting it with a rock star. Seeing the women backstage, Joe had to be busting at the seams.

Melody glanced at Joe. Absorbed in a video game, he had no clue that for the past thirty minutes she'd been trying to get his attention. She'd fluffed and played with her hair, pulling it over her shoulder. When that didn't work, she seductively stretched, making sure her t-shirt lifted enough to show off her stomach. Her subtle attempts to seduce Joe were pathetic compared to the zombie apocalypse playing out on the television.

Yeah, she'd need to reach down into her bag of tricks and pull something out from Girls Gone Wild. But that was the problem, she didn't play games. Trying to be sexy made her feel uncomfortable and, quite frankly, silly. She wasn't like the girls backstage with fake boobs, hourglass bodies, and Botox lips. She'd seen the way groupies worked. It was no different than when she was on tour with her dad years ago.

She looked down at her boobs. *"Well, girls, it's showtime."*

Melody shut down the laptop, then sauntered over to the sliding door that separated the bunks from the back of the bus. She closed it quietly, then turned to Joe. It didn't faze him. He was still immersed in the game. She rolled her eyes.

Tugging off her black Gracefall tee, she wadded it up and threw it at him, knocking the controller out of his hands. She stood with her hand on her hips, praying her hot-pink lace bra and black boy shorts looked sexy.

A huge smile spread across his face. "Hey there."

"Hey." Her body heated instantly against his smoldering gaze. The pink bra had done the trick. With newfound confidence in her step, she sauntered toward him.

He sat up, sitting on the edge of the couch. Out of his reach, she turned around, giving him the full shot of her ass.

She hooked her thumbs inside the waistband of her shorts and slowly slid them off her hips. God, she hoped she was doing this right.

Melody looked over her shoulder, shooting Joe a playful grin. The desire in his eyes turned her on. "Do you want more, Rock Star?"

"Fuck yeah." He reached for her, and she moved out of the way.

"Impatient, are we?" She slowly bent over, removing her shorts.

"Fuck!" he hissed as she turned around in her hot-pink thong.

He lunged forward and wrapped his arms around her waist, pulling her toward him. His breath was hot against her stomach. "You're the most beautiful woman I've ever seen." He kissed her navel.

She pushed him back on the couch. "I wasn't going for beautiful. I was going for Girls Gone Wild." She straddled him, her breasts inches from his face.

"Baby, you've achieved that." He slipped her bra strap off her shoulder and kissed the tops of her breasts, which spilled out of her bra. The coarseness of his beard on her skin sent a shiver down her spine.

His touch, his kiss, the way he looked at her like she was the only girl in the world made her feel sexy...beautiful. However, she was in control of this show. She clasped her hands on his bearded jaw, tearing him away from the delicious torture. They locked eyes, and nothing else mattered in the world. It was her and him.

Melody leaned in and kissed him. Her tongue slipped past his lips and danced with his perfectly, like the first night he'd kissed her. Heat smoldered deep inside as his grip tightened around her, crushing her body to his. The kiss deepened, and a buzz rushed through her like she'd been hit by lightning. This was the feeling that turned good girls bad.

She broke free to catch her breath. "Joe Grace, I do believe you can kiss a girl stupid."

A wicked grin spread across his face, and that was all it took to lure her in. She placed a kiss on his cheek, to his ear, and down his neck. Good God, his woodsy scent drove her wild. He leaned back, relishing in her kisses.

"Baby," he sighed. "Keep kissing my neck like that, and some shit is going down." His strong hands slid down her back to her ass. He squeezed it, pushing her against his arousal.

It empowered her, knowing he liked what she was doing. She licked her way up to his ear. "That's kinda my plan." She took his earlobe between her teeth and gave it a small tug.

Melody reached down and pulled his shirt off. Before the tee hit the floor, he had her lying on her back with him on top of her. Pulling her bra down, he squeezed, licked, and kissed her breasts. She sucked in a breath as his tongue swirled around her stiff nipple. Desire highjacked her mind as she fell deeper and deeper under his seductive spell. She wrapped her arms around him, loving the feel of his muscled body against hers. "You feel amazing."

He released her nipple and looked up at her. Lustful, steel-gray eyes stirred her desire. "Baby, I'm just getting started." He kissed her neck. "I've waited a long time to have you. I'm taking my time."

His kisses drove her wild. She turned her head to the side, marveling in the softness of his lips. "Don't make me wait too long, Rock Star," she panted.

He slipped his hand inside her panties and palmed her sex, dipping his finger along her sensitive flesh, teasing her.

She wrapped her leg around his waist, giving him full access.

"Mel," he hissed. "You're so fucking hot."

She heard a rip, then felt freed from her thong. "Please tell me you didn't rip my underwear."

A hot-pink flash flew past her. "I'll buy you another pair." He winked as he slid down and hooked his arm under her thigh. Hot kisses seared her skin as he worked his way to her sex. Every touch, lick, and nip sent a buzz rushing through her body.

With the first swirl of his tongue over her clit, she knew she was in trouble. The torture was sweet. He pushed into an exotic rhythm, never skipping a beat. The sensation was too much. She wiggled away, fighting the pleasure.

"Where are you going?" He smirked as he pulled her back, bringing her sex back to his mouth.

"Joe," she moaned, trying to protest, but she couldn't. She wanted more. "Oh, god," she sighed as he sucked her clit, fucking her with his tongue.

Slow and steady strokes melted her into a pool of desire. She wasn't one to beg, but holy hell, what she would give to have him inside her right now.

As if he'd read her mind, he slipped a finger inside her. She gasped and arched off the couch. He licked her, fucked her, keeping up with the rocking of her hips and making her give him everything she had.

A wave of pleasure washed over her. She was coming.

Pulse pounding, she was exploding. She gripped his hair. "Joe, I'm—oh, fuck me," she panted and bucked against him as the first wave of her orgasm hit. Her brain went fuzzy as Joe controlled her body.

Every whimper and moan seemed to encourage him more, and he pushed her deeper into orgasm. She shattered again as he slipped another finger inside her. The pleasure was unlike anything she'd ever felt before, as if she were having an out-of-body experience.

No longer holding back, she wrapped herself around him as she shattered into a million beautiful pieces.

He slid up her naked body, his tattooed chest wet with sweat. He kissed her neck right below her earlobe, almost causing her to come again. "So fucking hot."

Breathless, she licked her lips. "Not sure why we waited this long."

"Right?" He hovered over her, brushing her hair back. "The sounds you make when you come drive me wild." He bent down and kissed her.

"Maybe I should repay the favor." Tattooed muscles flexed beneath her touch as she slid her hands down his chest to the waistband of his jeans. She popped the button open while kissing him with a hunger she'd never felt before.

"I don't think I'll last long with your hands on me."

"Who said I was using my hands."

The door from the bunks slid open. "Hey." Tyler poked his head in. "We're stopping to eat. Oh shit! I'm sorry."

She hid beneath Joe's big body as he lay on his side, shielding her from his bandmate. "What the fuck, T! Knock much?" Joe shouted.

"Sorry. I wasn't thinking...you know...the two of you... banging... Shit, I'll just stop." Tyler backed away and into Dylan.

Dylan peeked over Tyler's shoulder. He laughed. "About fucking time, you two." A sly smile spread across his face.

"Go away!" Joe grabbed a pillow and threw it at them. "Close the door."

Mel peeked over Joe's huge bicep. "We'll be ready in two seconds."

As Tyler was sliding the door closed, she heard Dylan yell, "Make it quick, I don't want to lose our reservation."

She sat up, looking for her shirt, shorts, and bra, finally locating them across the room. She padded over and picked them up. "This was really irresponsible of me." She tugged on her shorts and bra. "I'm your tour manager."

"Hey." He pulled her onto his lap. "The guys know we're a thing." He kissed her shoulder.

"Still, my job is being a manager, not your—"

"Girlfriend?" He wrapped his arms around her as if he never wanted to let her go.

She faced him. "This is silly. I feel like I'm a groupie or something." She looked down, avoiding Joe's gaze.

"Mel, it's not like that."

"I know." She shook her head. "You know how hard this lifestyle is for me to accept. I just don't want to see it destroy us."

He cupped her face, bringing her eyes to his. "I would never allow anything to happen to us. You're all I want."

She wanted to believe, by God, she did. But she knew all too well rock and roll would be the death of their relationship.

"Hey." He caressed her cheek. "I will prove you wrong. I can have you and my music."

"And I want you to have it all, Joe. You've worked your ass off. You deserve success. The whole band does."

"Then stop overthinking things." He leaned in and kissed her softly.

His lips, his teasing tongue in her mouth, made her forget about the inevitable. This was Joe, her best friend, and now lover. She wasn't afraid of him hurting her, but rock and roll would destroy her.

"We should get dressed." She played with the ends of her long blond hair.

He pulled her close, crushing her against him. "You know what?"

"What?"

"I can't stop thinking about how incredible it's going to be when we finally bang."

"Bang?" She raised a brow. "You actually refer to sex as banging?"

"Yep." He nipped at her shoulder. "I can't wait to have you."

"I don't know," she teased. "Banging on a tour bus full of rock stars feels a little groupie-ish to me."

"Don't worry." He winked. "I have it all planned out." He slapped her ass. "Go get dressed. I'm hungry."

11

*T*he day started with the hustle and bustle of putting together a rock show, which included a pre-show meet and greet. Melody stood on stage underneath the mid-afternoon Florida sun, waiting for the stage manager. The Florida heat was much like California in August, hot and humid. Palm trees lined the outdoor stadium and swayed in the gulf breeze. She sighed. Life on the road made a Cali girl yearn for home.

Driving sixteen hours multiple times a week had taken a toll on everyone. More times than not, she'd had to remind the guys what day it was and where they were. Every show was exhausting, from setup to break down to packing up and heading to the next town. Gracefall gave it their all, pouring their heart and soul into every song, rocking all the way to the nosebleeds. The guys were made for rock and roll. She was not.

Attending parties with Joe had been fun at first, but now she hated walking into a hotel room, strung out from the road with all eyes on her. She'd missed the normalcy of regular life. She missed her dad and Dani like crazy. Even missed her mom.

Not telling her mom about her new adventure before she'd left had been a good strategy. When she did call, her mom went ballistic, chastising her about how irresponsible her decision had been to go on the road with a rock band. Thank God for the mute button. She didn't dare confess she'd fallen in love with Joe.

Her mother's voice nagged inside her brain.

"Why did you walk away from the orchestra to follow a band?" The disappointment in her mother's voice still cut her deeply.

"The rock scene is no place for a good girl." Yeah, that one deserved an eye roll. What mom didn't know about her little girl...

"What about your dreams?" And right there, the doubt was set in like a seed ready to sprout.

Joe was living his dream, and she was proud of him. But to say she wasn't a little envious would be a lie. She wanted her dream, too.

She'd never imagined falling in love with Joe. He was her best friend. Looking back, she always knew she had feelings for him. He knew her. The real her. Inside and out. He got her. Completely.

When he wasn't Mr. Rock Star, and when they were alone, there was a different side of Joe she'd fallen for. It was in the silence she felt solace, cuddling in his bunk listening to his heartbeat. It was in the depths of his steel-gray eyes that she knew he loved her. But was love enough?

Shaking free from doubt, she opened her notebook, looking over the to-do list that kept growing. She was in no mood to obsess over her life decisions. Her inner cheerleader took over. She was managing a tour for Gracefall. Joe

Grace, the uber-sexy drummer, was in love with her. What could go wrong?

"Hey, Boss Lady." Gary walked across the stage with a toothpick in his mouth. He was an older man in his fifties with thick silver and black hair. "You wanted to see me?"

"Yeah. Tonight's show is sold out. Seventy-thousand fans." She looked at her watch. "In four hours, the stadium will be filled. This is the biggest show to-date, and nothing can go wrong."

Gary folded his arms. "I've been doing this for a long time. You have nothing to worry about." He winked. "Come, I'll show you."

Relieved, she followed him to the lighting rig. Finally, something was going right.

Her cell vibrated in the back pocket of her cutoff jean shorts. She excused herself and took the call. It was Joe.

"Hey," she answered. "Everything okay?"

"Um, we have a problem in the green room. The makeup artist is a no-show, Dylan is threatening to wear a leather jacket with fringe, and Kimmy is having a total meltdown."

Kimmy rode the edge of having a nervous breakdown every time one tiny thing was out of whack. Melody looked down at her watch. Shit. In less than an hour the band was scheduled for their pre-show meet and great. "Tell Kimmy to go grab my toiletry bag from the bus and to breathe. I'll be right there."

"Sure thing, Boss Lady." What was with the Boss Lady nickname? She shook her head, listening to the muffled relaying of her message to Kimmy. "She said she's on it."

"Great." She motioned to Gary that she had to go, and he waved her off. She hustled offstage toward the green room, passing busy roadies setting up for tonight's show.

"You want to know something?" Joe's voice was low and

deep, turning her attention away from the dressing room disaster and onto the sexy man over the phone.

"What?"

"I'm picturing you naked."

Heat rose through her body to her cheeks. "Is that so?"

"Uh huh. It's the most productive thing I've done all day."

"Well, we'll have to fix that. I can think of a few things to keep you busy." Her grin was so wide her cheeks hurt.

"Fill my schedule. I'm all yours."

She wished it were true, but the reality was his schedule was already full. She wouldn't have any alone time with him until New York. Thank God they were flying out in the morning. "I'm right down the hall. See you in a second."

As she hung up, she reached the green room, flashed her pass to security, and was let in.

"Hey." She tossed her bag and notebook on the table. "Is Kimmy back?"

Joe greeted her with a kiss. "Not yet."

"Okay." Melody stepped out of his embrace and went straight to work. "Dylan, the eighties hair bands called, they want their leather, fringe jacket back."

"What?" Dylan stood with his arms stretched out, making the white fringe dance. "I'm bringing glam back, baby."

"No, the jacket goes." She turned to Mox, who played his guitar softly in the background, watching the shitshow unfold. He was still wearing a two-day-old shirt. "Moxie, change your shirt."

"Yes, ma'am." He set his guitar down and tugged his shirt off. Melody tossed him a bottle of deodorant and a clean shirt.

She turned her attention to Tyler. "Ty, if you're wearing leather pants, off with the underwear."

He stood and examined his pants. "What?"

"You'll need these." Joe threw a pair of wadded-up socks at him.

"Fuck you." Tyler threw the socks back and grabbed his dick. "I've got plenty right here."

Before the banter continued, she faced Joe and raised a brow. "Enough. Sit down." She grabbed a brush. "Your hair is out of control."

"As you wish." He sat in a chair in front of the mirror, which was lined in round blinding light bulbs. He pulled her between his legs so her breasts were eye level. His hands moved up her thighs to her waist.

She glared at him. "Behave."

Downtime led to boredom, and boredom always led to chaos.

Kimmy rushed in, panting and holding Melody's makeup bag. "I ran as fast as I could." Her long black hair was stuck around her neck from sweat.

"Thanks, Kimmy." She took the bag and found some foundation, powder, and black eyeliner. That's all a rock star needed, right?

"Jesus," Kimmy exclaimed. "We have thirty minutes to get to the pre-show meet and greet." She paced the small room. "We're going to be late."

Kimmy's nervousness was giving Melody a major headache. "Calm down. We'll be fine." Everyone would be fine if Kimmy left. "Hey, you should go check out the meet and greet setup. You know, do your thing, make sure everything is there for the guys, like water on the table."

"Yeah, that's a good idea. Thanks, Mel."

"No problem."

Kimmy left, and with her went all the anxiety in the room.

Melody took in a deep breath and returned her focus on Joe's makeup. She took out her foundation. Joe stopped her. "No makeup."

"But I thought—"

"Nope. That's Dylan."

Dylan walked over. Thank God without the fringe jacket. He rummaged through her makeup bag. "Got any black eyeliner, Mellie?"

"Yeah, side pocket."

"Got it." He leaned in toward the mirror and outlined his eyes with the pencil.

"Wow." She took a closer look at Dylan applying makeup. "You're pretty good at that."

He shrugged a shoulder. "When we first started out, we did our own makeup."

"Hey," Tyler interrupted. "Remember the Halloween show we did at The Roxy when we dressed up like Kiss?"

Joe sighed, "Don't remind me."

"What?" Dylan teased. "You don't want Mel to know you wore platform shoes that night and fell off the stage."

Mox laughed. "You busted your ass."

"And smeared your makeup," Tyler added as he walked over and handed a picture to Melody.

"No, no, no! Give me that." Melody kept Joe from snatching the photo. She looked at it. "Oh. My. God!"

Everyone in the room, except for Joe, was laughing.

The band was dressed up like Kiss, with big hair, black and white makeup, all of it. The guys were sweaty, like the picture had been taken after the show. And there was Joe.

The black makeup had run into the white, leaving gray streaks down his face. And then there were the platform shoes. "Oh, babe." She looked at him, holding back laughter.

"Screw you guys!" He grabbed the picture and tossed it in the garbage.

She felt bad for laughing, but she wasn't letting this one go. Not after he'd teased her for weeks for dancing on the bar. "Don't be mad. I can't walk in platforms either." She laughed.

"Okay. That's enough. I got it. Ha-ha, joke's on Joe." Scowling, he sat down in the chair.

Melody walked over and sat on his lap. He wouldn't look at her. "I think hot mess looks good on you."

"Now you know why I don't wear makeup."

"Good call."

He looked at her and grinned.

"I knew you couldn't stay mad at me." She returned a smile.

He cupped her face. "No, I could never stay mad at you." He kissed her.

Instant butterfly flutters.

"Okay, lovebirds," Mox interrupted. "Kimmy's going to have a heart attack if we don't get to the meet and greet soon. Let's go."

Steel-gray eyes stared into hers. "We'll finish this later."

His voice melted her insides. "I'll hold you to it, Rock Star."

He kissed her quickly and smacked her ass. "Showtime."

They filed out of the room, and she had them backstage waiting for their meet and greet with ten minutes to spare. She gazed out into the stadium. The front section was filled with fans wearing their Gracefall gear and holding signs. It was the largest crowd she'd seen since she'd joined the tour.

"Babe," she called Joe over. "Do you see this?"

He stood behind her, looking out at the fans. "Holy shit."

"I know, right?" She turned around and hugged him. "You made it, Rock Star."

"I always knew we'd make it, but never expected this." The surprise in his voice brought tears to her eyes.

She stepped out of his embrace and distracted herself from crying by smoothing the creases from his shirt. "Gracefall deserves this. You deserve it."

Gazing deep into her eyes, he took her hand away from his t-shirt and kissed it. "Don't cry. We do deserve this."

She smiled. "They're happy tears." She wiped a fallen tear from her cheek.

"Gracefall!" Kimmy shouted over the roaring cheers, interrupting their tender moment. "You're on!"

"Knock 'em dead." She raised on her tiptoes and kissed his cheek. She was so proud of him and happy to see his fans excited to meet the band. His dreams were coming true, and how lucky was she to witness it all?

He brushed his thumb over her bottom lip. The coarseness of his skin sent a bolt of lightning down her spine. One touch, and she wanted him. "I'll be picturing you naked." He smiled.

She tamped down the desire racing through her body. "You're so bad."

"I know." He bent down and claimed her lips. "See you soon." He let her go and joined the band on stage for the pre-show meet and greet.

As soon as he left, the storm of doubt rolled in. She crossed her arms over her chest, giving herself some comfort. A dark cloud hovered over them. Why was she waiting for the storm instead of living in this beautiful moment?

Because the very thing Joe worked so hard for would eventually destroy them. The longer she stayed with Joe, the harder she would fall. Was Joe worth the broken heart?

She watched Joe as he took the stage. The fans went wild as Dylan, Joe, Moxley, and Tyler walked out, waving to the crowd. The throng of maniacs jumped out of their seats and chanted, "Gracefall...Gracefall...Gracefall..." In the front row, groupies jumped up and down, flashing their tits, desperate to get their attention. Security held back a rush of music journalists, from top YouTubers to podcasters chomping at the bit to ask questions. Everyone wanted a piece of them.

The guys took their seats behind a banquet table as the meet and greet host introduced the band. It took the beautiful brunette, who looked like she'd spent all day at the beach, a few minutes to calm the fans down and welcome the band to Florida. Joe turned on the rock star act, which wasn't as bad as Dylan's sexually infused answers to the host's questions. He'd even made her squirm in her seat a few times. Yeah, Melody would see her later on the bus.

Among the chaos, she needed to find a few minutes for herself. None of this was real. She refused to wrap herself in this insanity. Dating a rock star wouldn't go to her head. She needed normalcy. Something to keep her grounded to herself.

"Hey, Kimmy, can you make sure the boys get to the food tent after the meet and greet?" A smile crossed her lips. "I have something I need to do."

The PR rep looked at her as though she'd grown two heads. "You want me," she pointed at herself, "to corral these wildlings to the food tent? You must be on drugs. No way." She shook her head and continued to watch the interview.

"Please," Melody begged. "It won't be hard. There's food involved."

Kimmy stood her ground.

"I need to get away for a while," Melody pleaded. "It would mean a lot to me."

The nervous, raven-haired woman rocked back and forth on her heels as Melody broke her down. "Stop begging," she huffed. "I'll do it."

"Thank you!" She hugged Kimmy so hard they almost fell over.

Melody made her way backstage, looking for a quiet space to hide out for a while. There was no way she was going back to the bus. That was the last place she wanted to be.

Backstage was quiet, for now. She looked at her phone, checking the time. Yeah, this was the calm before tonight's show. The roadies were either at the food tent or taking a quick nap.

Melody passed a row of black instrument trunks with "Gracefall" stamped across it. A cello case caught her attention. Since when did Gracefall use a cello on stage? She walked over to the case and studied it for a moment. She hadn't played since that dreaded day she'd found out she failed the audition.

Excitement streaked through her as she popped open the case.

She took the instrument out, admiring its beauty. By the look of the richness of the wood, the cello was top-of-the-line quality. Her hands itched to play, but it wasn't hers. She didn't know who it belonged to, and she didn't want to run the risk of something happening to the instrument. It was better to just put it back.

As she began to place the cello back into its case, she paused. Surely, it needed to be tuned properly. Who better to do it than herself? Giving in to the temptation, she grabbed the bow and cello and looked for a place to play.

Melody found a smaller, shorter trunk that was the perfect height. She sat down and positioned the cello between her legs. She tuned the cello, playing through the scales with her left hand on the fingerboard and her right holding the bow.

The instrument played to perfection. Before she knew it, she was playing, "Can't Help Falling in Love." The Elvis song was her father's favorite and the first song she'd learned. They'd played together, her on the cello and him on the drums. She missed those simpler times.

Now, the song reminded her of Joe.

~

*J*oe walked backstage after he'd signed the last pair of tits. He loved meeting fans, but all he'd thought about was getting back to Mel. They had a couple hours before the show, and he wanted to spend them with her.

He'd been patient, understanding Mel didn't want their first time to be on a tour bus. Soon they would be in New York, alone in a hotel room. He had a surprise for her—he'd changed their reservations, upgrading her room to a luxury suite, and made dinner reservations. He'd even bought her something special. Everything was lined up for a perfect night she wouldn't forget.

He scanned the backstage area, looking for Mel. Where was she?

"Hey, Kimmy!" He grabbed her attention as she tried to corral the rest of the band backstage. "Have you seen Mel?"

"Yeah, I don't know where she went. She said she had something to do, then left me with this." The PR rep motioned to his bandmates, who were engaging with a group of fans fighting security to get backstage.

Kimmy didn't have the situation under control. If she didn't get the guys out of there, the fans were going to breach the security staff.

"Mel told me I wouldn't have any problems getting you guys to the food tent." She shrugged her shoulders. "I have no idea how to get their attention." She turned to him with a frown. "And I'm not flashing my boobs. I'm out."

Joe stopped her from walking away. He wolf-whistled over the screams, gaining his bandmates' attention. "Food!" he yelled.

The guys came running.

Kimmy looked up at him and mouthed, "Thank you."

He smiled. "No problem."

As they left for the food tent, Joe made his way through the backstage area. The stadium where they were playing was huge. He hoped he wouldn't get lost. On his way to find Mel, he passed a few stagehands catching a nap on top of equipment trunks that lined the hallway. The production manager strode by him, cussing someone out on the phone. But no sign of Mel. He pulled out his phone to text her when he heard a cello playing softly. His heart skipped a beat. He'd found Mel.

He followed the music, humming to the Elvis tune as the melody brought back a memory of his childhood—one of the good ones when he was with Mel. One night after a drum lesson at her house, he heard someone playing the cello. Just like now, he'd followed the music as it enchanted his soul. As a thirteen-year-old kid without a family to show him love, he didn't know much about it until that very moment as he watched a cute blonde-haired girl sitting behind a huge string instrument. Something strange had happened inside his chest that night as he stood mesmerized by each note she played with elegance and precision. She was the grace missing from his life.

He rounded the corner. There she was, sitting on a trunk with a cello between her long, tanned legs. Her eyes were closed, shutting the rest of the world out. She moved the bow across the stings elegantly as she lost herself in the music. Joe leaned against the wall with his arms crossed, watching her. He could do this for hours and never tire. It surprised him she hadn't made the orchestra—she was amazing.

She opened her eyes and saw him watching. She lowered the bow and stopped playing. "Hey." She grinned. "I couldn't resist."

She stood, and he stopped her. "Don't mind me. Keep playing."

Gently, she sat back down. "Okay." She positioned herself and continued.

He took a seat behind her, so she sat perfectly between his legs. Thank God the bench was sturdy—he was a big guy. He gathered her long blonde hair in his hand and brushed it off to the side, giving him access to her neck. A jasmine scent flooded his nose and went straight to his cock. Hell's bells, he loved this woman.

He nuzzled her neck, kissing and tasting her. He wrapped his arms around her waist and pulled her against him. She turned her head toward him. "How am I supposed to play with you distracting me?"

Joe let up on the kisses. "Concentrate. You're the schooled musician." He kissed her cheek and trailed back down her neck.

She cleared her throat. "This is so unfair."

He smiled as she continued to play "Can't Help Falling in Love."

Joe slipped his hands up her shirt, admiring her soft, smooth skin. Reaching the bottom of her bra, he felt her suck in a shaky, anticipating breath. He took her earlobe gently between his lips, teasing it with light kisses. "You feel amazing."

A petite moan escaped her. "I'm getting the feeling you're enjoying distracting me." She pressed her ass against his cock.

"Fuck," he sighed.

"Two can play that game."

"Yeah, but your hands are busy playing the cello." He shoved his hands under her bra and cupped her tits. "Mine are busy playing you."

Mel continued to play without skipping a beat.

Her nipples hardened as he squeezed and teased, still kissing gently down her neck.

He upped the stakes and moved one of his hands down her stomach, crossing the state line. She leaned back as he slid his hands under her panties, feeling her hot, wet heat. "Baby, you're so fucking hot." He slipped a finger between her slick folds, stroking her lightly up and down.

Her bow squeaked across the cello strings.

"Melody Sterling," he said against her ear. "Your bow hand is slipping."

Mel dropped the bow. "Game over." She laid the cello

down. "You won." She straddled him, claiming his lips in wild hunger.

Carnal need pulsed through him as she shoved her hands in his hair. He pushed his hands down the back of her cutoffs, squeezing her ass, pressing her against his hard-aching dick. There was nothing more he wanted right now than to be inside her, feeling her sex sliding against his dick.

"Maybe our first time should be on the tour bus." She thrust her hips forward. "Joe, I need you," she whispered breathlessly against his lips.

Did he hear her right? She attacked his neck with kisses. Oh yeah, he did. "I have two hours before the show." He winked.

"I'll take it."

Joe stood before she had a chance to change her mind and picked her up over his shoulder in true caveman fashion. He didn't care. He was crazy with need.

"Joe," she laughed, "I'm going with you willingly. No need to knock me over the head and drag me back to the cave."

He nipped her thigh. "Me, Joe. You, Mel."

She playfully slapped his ass, and he loved the feel of her hands on his body.

His feet weren't moving fast enough, or time was standing still, because it took forever to get to the bus. He swung the door open, almost breaking it off its hinges.

He put her down, and their lips came together with hungered passion—a passion built up and ready to explode. He kicked the door closed, slamming the damn thing so hard it shook the bus.

Kissing down her neck, he lifted her shirt. She leaned her head back, marveling in his kisses. "Are we really doing this?"

He cupped her face, gazing at her pink, full lips, imagining their sweet torture on his body. "Fuck yeah, we are." A wicked grin spread across his face.

"Dylan, is that you?" A woman's voice came from the back of the bus.

Joe's world halted. He recognized the voice but didn't understand why she was here.

He stepped out of Mel's embrace and instinctually hid her behind him. The woman slithered down the hallway like the snake she was. He wasn't buying the front she put on, wearing mom jeans and a Gracefall rock tee as though she was a supportive mom. His jaw locked in anger. "Why are you here?"

"Hi, Joe. I was expecting Dylan."

"Sorry to disappoint." He folded his arms, standing firm. "Now get off my bus."

Joe ignored Mel's tap on his shoulder. He couldn't believe it. After all these years, now was the time he'd have to explain his demon bitch of a mother to Mel. No. Karen was as good as dead to him. Mel wouldn't be dragged into this dark part of his life. He'd fought too hard to break free from this woman to allow her back in now.

He took a step toward his mom. "I don't know who let you on the bus, but you're not welcome here. Get. Out."

The woman set her eyes on Mel. "Is that Melody Sterling?" She held her hand out. "I'm Karen Grace, Joe's mother."

Mel moved out from behind Joe. "I can't believe I'm finally meeting your mother, Joe."

He stopped her as she reached to shake his mother's hand. "Don't touch it. You don't know where it's been."

Mel retracted her hand. Confusion swept over her face as she looked up at him. "But, it's your mom."

"Mel, stay out of this," he warned.

"If you want me gone," Karen held out her hand as though asking for a handout, "I need money for the bus."

"And the truth will set you free!' He threw his hands up sarcastically. "Of course, you do. That's why you're here. You're out of money. You're not here to support your kids." His steel-gray eyes narrowed in on her.

Joe didn't want Mel to see him like this, but this woman brought out the demon in him. He took his wallet from his back pocket, opened it, and took out a hundred-dollar bill. He leaned in close to Karen, so Mel couldn't hear what he was about to say. "Take it." He placed the bill in her hand. "Make sure you get the good stuff."

He'd become numb to her drug habit. He'd seen the repetitive destructive behavior ruin his mother. Joe wasn't naïve to the promise of the last high, nor did he hang onto hope that one day his mother would get clean and stay clean. This was something he'd stopped trying to fix a long time ago. His heart no longer ached for her.

Joe opened the bus door. "Don't come back."

Without an ounce of shame, his mother took the money and walked off the bus.

He hung his head, taking in a few calming breaths. He should text Dylan and warn him. Knowing Karen, she'd hit him up next. He took his cell from his back pocket and began to text when he heard Mel clear her throat.

He looked up from his cell and met her beautiful hazel eyes. He wanted to hold her and tell her everything. His mother's drug addiction, his messed-up childhood home, which was nothing more than a whore house with revolving doors, spinning with men coming and going. Then there was his brother. He didn't need a Ph.D. in psychology to know where Dylan was heading.

"I'm speechless, Joe."

"Good, because there's nothing to talk about." He strode into the kitchen and took a beer out of the refrigerator.

She followed him. "Are you serious? Your mother took time away from her patients and travel to come to see you and you treated her like garbage."

The irony of it all made him a chuckle inside. Yep, she'd taken time away from her patients all right—a different kind of patient. He leaned against the counter and tossed back his beer. "Mel, it's complicated. I don't want to talk about it."

"Do you not trust me?"

"Jesus, Mel, leave it be." He'd never raised his voice to her—ever.

She took a step back. "I'm your girlfriend. I have every right to know."

She was right, but he had every right to keep his lie. The past would stay hidden in the gutter, along with his mother.

"I'm sorry." He pulled her into a hug that she resisted. He tried to kiss her, but she turned away, leaving him kissing her cheek. Shit, how was he going to get out of this without telling her the truth? If he had the balls, he'd tell her now. However, coming from an abusive childhood and being poor wasn't something he was proud of, nor talked about. Mel came from money. Her parents were divorced, but they loved her. She was accustomed to higher standards—more than he could give her, until now.

He'd made something of himself and could give her whatever her heart desired—except for the truth.

Joe looked at his watch. "Shit. I have to go."

Mel crossed her arms over her chest. The expression on her face told him this wasn't over. "Are you coming to the show?"

"No, I think I'll sit this one out."

"What if I said I'll be imagining you naked while I'm on stage tonight." He tried to lighten her mood.

Her lips raised in a tender half-smile. "I'd say you better focus on keeping the beat."

"Baby, I have no problem with that."

Joe exited the bus. The conversation was far from over, but he'd dodged the bullet for now.

12

*F*inally, Melody was off the tour bus and heading to New York on the record company's private jet. The night before had been awkward between her and Joe. He'd avoided any further discussion about his mother by inviting their opening act, Whiplash, on the bus to celebrate for an after-show party. Joe wasn't the rowdy type; however, partying with the wild guys from Whiplash had brought out a different side of him, the side she was pretending didn't exist—the obnoxious, drunken rock star.

Whiskey flowed like water, and egos got big. She'd left the bus in the middle of a heated Battle of the Bands competition between Dylan and Jake, the lead vocalist for Whiplash. She hadn't cared who could hit the high note higher—she'd wanted to sleep.

But what bothered her the most...Joe hadn't noticed she had left. She'd returned to find him passed out.

Seriously, she was so done hanging around these boys. They were driving her crazy. Living on the bus was driving her crazy. She was ready for the five-day break in New York. Even though there were two shows booked and a birthday bash for Davidson it was still a break from the bus. Staying at a posh hotel in her own room with a king-sized bed, fluffy, oversized pillows, and a do not disturb sign sounded like heaven. No boys allowed. Well, maybe one boy.

She looked at the big guy sitting next to her, sleeping with his AirPods in his ears. She couldn't stay mad at him for long. This was his rock and roll life. She was along for the ride.

Melody scooted next to Joe and slipped her arm around his, then laid her head on his shoulder. She closed her eyes and took in his fresh, clean scent. God, he smelled good.

"Does this mean you're not mad at me anymore?" His voice was raspy from sleep.

"I wasn't mad."

"So, this morning, when I said good morning and you told me to fuck off, you weren't mad at me?"

Melody cringed. She'd been tired and cranky and yeah, a little pissed. But she didn't mean for him to hear what she'd said under her breath, "You heard that?"

"Oh yeah, I was picking up what you were putting down."

"I'm sorry." She looked up at him, resting her chin on his broad shoulder. She gently ran her finger down his tattooed neck. "Forgive me?"

"Baby, I'm the one who should be asking for forgiveness."

She teased him, batting her eyelashes at him, waiting for his apology.

He turned in his seat to face her. "Sorry, I was a douchebag last night." She was pulled in close until her forehead was touching his. "I'll make it up to you," he whispered huskily.

Joe teased her lips with his, giving her a naughty version

of the warm and fuzzies. If they weren't landing soon, she'd ask to be a member of the mile-high club. "So." She cleared her throat. "What did you have in mind?"

"Five days alone in New York." Hunger burned in his depths as he gazed deep into her eyes. Her body lit up like the Fourth of July. "You, me...that's all I need."

"Sounds like a plan." She smiled as she leaned in and kissed him.

"Holy shit!" Mox's voice rang out from the back of the jet, breaking their kiss.

Melody looked up to find Mox walking down the aisle toward them.

"Sam's in labor!"

Joe shot up from the seat. "Holy shit, dude!"

Sweat rolled down Mox's face. "I need to get off this fucking plane and get to my wife." He paced the aisle.

"Moxley, calm down." Melody turned around and kneeled in her seat so she could see Mox. "This is her first baby. Labor could last a long time."

Mox plopped down in the seat behind her. "It's a good thing we're heading to New York. As soon as we land, I'm heading to the hospital."

"How far along are her contractions?" Melody asked.

"I didn't ask." Mox leaned back in the seat. "Sam told me she was in labor. I panicked. I said I'd be right there and hung up."

Joe sat down next to Mox. "Well, maybe if you were Superman."

"Or we could just give him the emergency parachute," Dylan said from across the aisle. "I'll jump with ya, bro. I've always wanted to skydive."

"How about we throw him out of the plane." Tyler, apparently grouchy from being woken up, yawned.

Melody shot them each a glare. "How about we go to the hospital with you, Mox. Moral support."

"Absolutely, bro," Joe said. "We'll be there."

Mox shoved his hand through his hair. "I was supposed to be home when this happened."

"Don't blame yourself," Melody reassured him. "Babies come when they're ready to. Trust me."

Joe's brows pinched together. "Since when did you become an expert on babies? You were a music major. Is there something you're not telling me?"

Melody rolled her eyes hard enough that she could feel them in the back of her head. "I'm a girl. We know these things."

Joe shrugged. "Just checking."

More like teasing her. It had always been his favorite thing to do. Test how far he could go before her cheeks turned red with embarrassment.

The pilot came on over the intercom announcing they would be landing soon.

Melody turned back around in her seat and fastened her seatbelt. "Mox," she called over her shoulder. "The offer still stands."

She felt his hand on her shoulder. "Thanks, Mellie Girl, but I'll be fine once we land and I'm on my way to the hospital. I'll call you guys when he or she gets here." He got up and went back to his seat.

Joe took his seat next to her. He leaned in and whispered in her ear. "In a selfish kind a way, I'm glad he doesn't want us to go to the hospital."

"Why?" The way he was rubbing her arm with a feather-like caress and kissing her ear lobe, she knew exactly what was on his mind.

"You'll see." He wriggled his brows.

The jet hit the runway, its wheels screeching on the tarmac. Melody held onto Joe's arm, closing her eyes tight as the plane slowed to a stop.

"Hey." Joe shook her arm. "We've landed. All is good."

Melody's eyes popped open as she pried her hand from Joe's forearm. She exhaled. They were on the ground. She could finally breathe again.

Joe stood and grabbed their carry-on bags from the overhead compartment. "I didn't know you were afraid of flying."

"I'm not." She cleared her throat as she stood. "Landings make me nervous."

"That's cute, Sterling." He flashed her a teasing smile.

She shook her head and followed him off the jet.

Outside, a black Suburban SUV waited for them. The driver opened the door for them, then loaded the vehicle with their luggage. The Suburban was spacious inside, seating at least seven. She sat in the middle of Joe and Dylan. Mox sat shotgun, strumming his fingers on his thighs, and Tyler had the backseat all to himself.

After they'd arrived at the hotel, Moxley talked the driver into dropping him off at the hospital. The band's schedule had worked out perfectly so Mox could be home for the birth of his child. He and Sam lived in Albany, and the hospital was only thirty minutes from the hotel.

As the last piece of luggage was loaded on the cart, the Suburban pulled out on the road, disappearing into traffic.

The bricked archways in front of the hotel made it look historic. It wasn't until Melody looked all the way up that she could see how massive it truly was. She stopped counting the stories when she reached thirty.

Through the revolving glass doors and to the left, a mahogany bar stood. Round tables that sat four each dotted the area in front. To her right, with matching decor, was the reception desk. Two beautiful women stood with smiles on their faces.

"Welcome to Albany. My name is Candy. How can I assist you?"

The woman looked well put together. Bleach blonde hair pulled tight and high on her head. Navy blue suit freshly pressed. The red scarf she wore around her neck matched the color of her lips. "Yes, we have a reservation under—"

"Let me take care of this." Joe stepped up to the desk. He folded his arms and rested them on the counter, shooting a smoldering glare at the woman.

Dylan stood next to Melody, watching his big brother. "He does this every time."

"What do you mean?" She asked, but did she really want to know?

"You'll see." Dylan looked down at her and grinned.

Joe looked back at little bro and hushed him with a finger to his lips.

"Can I get your name, sir?" Candy asked as if she was running out of patience.

Joe turned back around. "Why, yes, you may. Hugh G. Rection."

The receptionist typed in the name, scanning the computer screen. "I'm sorry, sir, I don't see a Hugh G. Rection."

"That's what she said." Dylan snickered through his hand, covering his mouth.

Melody felt her face redden with embarrassment for the woman.

Joe leaned over the counter, trying to get a look at the screen. "Are you sure you don't see a Hugh G. Rection?"

"Oh, wait," Candy looked up from her screen. "I found it."

"Great!" Joe slapped his hands on the counter. "I was beginning to worry."

Dylan busted into laughter. "He kills me every time with this shit."

After checking in, they headed to the elevators and waited.

Melody glared at Joe.

"What?" He shrugged.

"Really? Huge erection?"

"Don't be mad, Mellie." Dylan put his arm around her. "It's a band ritual. Every hotel we stay in, we give prank names."

The elevator doors opened, and they filed in.

"I'm not mad." Melody rolled her eyes. "Cranky, yes. I need sleep."

"I'm not sure you'll be sleeping." Tyler nodded to Joe. "Mr. Hugh G. Rection needs attention."

"Fuck yeah, dude." Dylan high-fived Tyler.

"All right." Joe read her don't-mess-with-me expression perfectly. "Joke has gone too far."

Melody leaned back against the cold steel elevator wall and shook her head. "Freaking man-child," she said under her breath.

Finally, the elevator stopped on the twentieth floor. Dylan and Tyler left first. As she began to follow, Joe pulled her back into the elevator and closed the doors.

"What are you doing?" Big arms wrapped around her.

"I told you I have a surprise."

"Elevator sex?"

"No, but good idea."

"Then what?"

The elevator stopped again. "You'll see."

They walked out and turned right down a long hallway. "Joe, why are we here? Our rooms are down a floor."

He stopped outside of room number 2015 and slid the key card in. It flashed green, then opened the door. Melody followed him in. He turned on the lights, and her luggage was already inside. "What is this?"

Vanilla, either candles or air freshener, wafted past her nose as she stepped inside. The coolness of the room gave her goosebumps. Crystal chandeliers resembling exploding fireworks hung throughout the suite, giving the room a warm glow. The walls were painted in thick gold and cream stipes. The suite opened to a spacious sitting area with a cream leather sofa and a matching chaise lounge chair. A crystal vase filled with red roses sat on the coffee table.

She turned to Joe. "Are we staying here?"

"You are."

"What do you mean?"

"I traded in my room and upgraded yours." He smiled. "I had the concierge pull some strings for me." He tipped his chin to the back bedroom. "Your bubble bath awaits."

Melody couldn't believe it. This suite was amazing, and she had it all to herself? "Where are you staying?"

"I'm crashing with Tyler and Dylan."

She sauntered toward Joe and placed her hand on his chest. "I'm better company. Stay here with me. Join me in the bubble bath."

"No, I promised myself I'd give you some alone time. Grab a nap, call room service, whatever you like."

"Are you sure?" She ran her hands down his chest.

He nodded. "Just be ready by eight o'clock."

"For what?"

He palmed her face, tracing his thumb over her lips. His steel-gray gaze set her on fire. "You're mine."

Disappointed, yet excited for tonight, she took a step back and shoved her hands in her cutoff jean short pockets. "Thank you for everything."

"No need to thank me. I want to take care of you." Joe kissed her on the cheek long enough to make her miss him. "I'll see you tonight." He winked and flashed her a wicked smile before leaving. The door closed, and her knees went weak. She leaned against the door. The cold steel pressed against her back, cooling her heated body. Being around Joe, she was always set ablaze.

Melody loved being alone with Joe without distractions, without feeling all eyes were on them. He was free to be the fun-loving boy she grew up with. He made her feel like she was the only girl in his life. But, since she'd been on the road with him, she'd seen a different side. What was he hiding from her? Why didn't he talk about his mother? Since she'd known him, every time his mom was mentioned, he'd shut her out or told her his mother was traveling. By now, she should have at least seen a picture of her. Why hadn't he introduced her to his mom on the bus? Something was wrong.

Now, she was curious. It all started when Joe shut Dylan up in the car when a childhood memory was mentioned. She'd thought nothing of it then—Dylan was drunk—but now there was something dark in Joe's past he didn't want her knowing. How was she supposed to let this go? If she loved Joe, which she did, she couldn't.

She peeled herself off the door. With a suitcase in tow, she headed to the bedroom to enjoy her bath. Maybe she was overthinking things. There had never been drama or problems in their friendship. He was the easiest person to talk to and get along with. Yes, grumpy at times, but aren't we all?

Everything is fine. Don't overthink Joe.

All her doubts washed away when she saw a large, white, rectangle box wrapped with a big red ribbon laying on the bed. A white envelope with her name on it was propped up in front of the box.

"Joe." A smile spread across her lips as she opened the letter.

Hey Baby,

I hope you like your gift. When I saw it, I thought of you. I can't wait to see you tonight—rooftop, 8:00. Don't be late.

Love you more than you know,

Rock Star

She laid the note down. *Joe, what have you done?*

Melody removed the ribbon, then popped the top off the box. Inside was pink tissue paper. She unfolded the paper and gasped. She took the garment out, holding it by its spaghetti straps. The light hit the dress just right, making the black sequins shimmer like diamonds.

She found a mirror and stood in front of it, holding the dress against her body. The deep V neckline stopped between her breasts. The dress came down to the top of her knees and slit high in the front. Melody turned from side to side. It was perfect. And best of all, he'd thought of her when he saw it.

She returned to the box, making sure she hadn't overlooked anything.

Joe had great taste.

Melody placed the little black dress on the bed, then went into the bathroom for her bath. She couldn't wait to see Joe's reaction to her in the dress. Tonight was going to be beyond amazing.

13

*J*oe stood on the rooftop of the hotel, looking down at his watch. Ten minutes more and Mel would be here. He rolled his shoulders, fidgeting to get comfortable in his suit jacket. Not even expensive Italian suits fit him perfectly. He checked his cuff links for the fiftieth time and rolled his neck, fidgeting in the suit.

Tonight was his first night alone with Mel. Everything had to be perfect. He'd started over an hour ago, making sure his preparations were complete. He'd checked in with the hotel chef, sampling tonight's dinner. Then he'd chatted with the wait staff about the table setting—the flowers had to be fresh. Finally, the hotel staff had had enough of him and suggested he go to the bar and get a drink.

Yeah, he was overthinking tonight, but hell, you only get one shot at your first time.

Joe walked over to the gazebo the hotel staff had put up for him. A round wicker daybed with cream covers and red fluffy pillows sat underneath. An inviting fire flickered in the pit in front of the bed. White lights lined the canopy and twinkled like stars. Everything was perfect. They could stay out here for the rest of the night without any distractions. Yeah, he wasn't getting cock blocked tonight.

"Hey, you."

Joe turned around, and Mel took his breath away. Words escaped him. He had never seen a more beautiful woman in his life. Her hair was tied up loosely in a side ponytail, giving him an unobstructed view of her neck and the dress's plunging neckline. The little black dress he'd bought looked stunning on her.

Melody turned around slowly. She stopped mid-turn and glanced over her shoulder at him. "Do you like it?"

Fuck yeah, he did. She was stunning. He wouldn't make it to dinner. "You're gorgeous."

She sauntered toward him. "So are you." She placed her hands on his chest, admiring the lapels of his jacket. "I've never seen you in a suit. Not even at prom."

Her sweet jasmine scent flooded his senses. He closed his eyes and breathed her in. Mel rendered him speechless.

"Is there something wrong?"

He opened his eyes to find her brows pinched together, matching the confusion in her voice. For fuck's sake, he needed to snap out of it. This was Mel, his best friend, his lover. "No, no." He shook his head, playing it off. "Nothing's wrong."

"Are you nervous?" Concern spread across her face as she took a step back. "I know this may all seem awkward. I mean, we're best friends. My dad thinks of you as a son. You've been like a—"

"If you say brother, I'm jumping off the fucking building."

Mel laughed. "I'm talking too much, aren't I?"

"Yes." He closed the distance between them, wrapping

his arm around her waist. "You do that when you're nervous." He caressed her cheek and gazed deep into her hazel, doe-like eyes. All his worries melted away like they did every time he was around her. "I'm not nervous. You took my breath away for a moment."

"To be honest, I'm so nervous right now."

"That's okay." Joe took her black clutch purse and laid it on the table. "Let's take it slow." He pulled out his cell phone, and a minute later, "Beast of Burden" by The Rolling Stones came on the little black speaker. He offered her his hand. "Dance with me?"

She answered with a smile that warmed his soul. "You know I can't resist this song."

He pulled her close, her body molding into his. She wrapped her arms around his neck, and he lost himself in her touch. Big hazel eyes looked up at him, and his heart skipped a beat. So innocent, beautiful, and all his.

Their hips swayed to the sensual beat, and their bodies moved together as if they were one. She teased the back of his neck with her fingertips. A comfortable silence fell between them as the song, their song, played on.

Joe slid his hands past her hips and squeezed her ass. The small moan coming from her lips about did him in. He trailed kisses down her neck to her shoulder. The thin black strap of her dress slid off her shoulder. Yeah, he wasn't waiting. He'd eat his dessert first. "Melody, I fucking need you now."

She looked over at the candlelit table set for two. "What about dinner?"

"Change of plans." He picked her up. "Let's work up an appetite first."

She threw her arms around his neck and claimed his lips.

Weeks of sexual tension snapped. He needed her like the air he breathed. He laid her down on the daybed, never breaking the kiss. In a hungered passion, he removed his jacket, throwing it across the floor.

Dickbrain kicked in. He needed to be inside her, feel her shatter from the orgasm he was going to give her. He'd waited a long time for this moment; he wouldn't hold back.

Buttons flew, seams popped as she ripped his shirt off. Surprised at her boldness, he looked down at her. Lust-filled eyes, swollen, red lips from his kisses, and boobs. He grinned. "Fuck yeah, baby."

She took his bottom lip between her teeth and softly tugged. "You turn me on."

Her confession went straight to his cock. He liked it.

She grabbed his ass, pulling his arousal harder against her. Joe sucked in a breath. He needed to start thinking about baseball before he struck out.

Sliding his hands up her thighs, he found the hem of her dress and worked it past her hips. He almost had his hands in her panties when her cellphone rang.

"Don't answer it," he growled into her neck between kisses.

"I have to," she sighed. "I'm sorry. I've been waiting for Kimmy to call about the press release for Saturday night's show. It will be quick."

He rolled off her. "Fuck," he groaned, frustrated.

∼

*M*elody pulled down her dress and made a mad dash to the table where her cell was going off like a siren. Shit. She should have left the damn thing in the room.

"Melody Sterling," she answered.

"Miss Sterling, this is Candy from the front desk."

What the—

"Hi, Candy from the front desk." She turned to Joe, confused. Did he have another surprise for her?

"It seems we have a problem." The annoyance in Candy's voice cut through the phone.

"What's the problem?" She had no idea what it could be. Maybe a credit card issue? But they weren't checking out for another four days.

"We've had multiple calls from our guests that a heavily tattooed man is running around our hotel naked. I'm assuming he's with the band."

Melody facepalmed. "Does he have a blond mohawk?"

"I do believe the woman in 1115 mentioned a mohawk and a very large," the receptionist cleared her throat, "member."

Oh my god! Mortified, she clasped her hand over her mouth.

"If you cannot handle this situation, we'll be forced to call the police, Miss Sterling."

"Candy, I'm so sorry. I'll take care of this immediately."

"Thank you. Enjoy your stay."

The phone went silent. *Damn it, Dylan!*

"I have to go." She grabbed her shoes.

"What?" Joe shot up from the bed.

"Your brother is running around the hotel naked. We have to find him before Candy calls the police."

"I'm going to fucking kill him." In a hurry, he put his shirt on, forgetting about the buttons that were left. "Do we know what floor he was last seen on?"

"No." She grabbed her purse and headed toward the

elevator. She couldn't believe her luck. Finally, she was alone with Joe, and Dylan was up to his old tricks.

They got into the elevator. She looked at Joe. Anger creased his brow as he stood with his arms crossed over his chest. She prayed she'd find Dylan before Joe. He was going to kill him, and she wouldn't blame him. This was their night. "Maybe we should start at the top and work our way down since we don't know where he is."

"Yep. I tried calling. No answer." He shrugged.

"I'm guessing his phone is with his clothes."

He faced her. "I don't care where his clothes are. We need to find him, so we can pick up where we left off."

His gaze shifted to her body, and her knees threatened to buckle. If she had ignored the call, she'd be experiencing that promise of pleasure in his eyes right now.

The elevator continued to descend, and Melody regained focus. "I'll take the odd floors; you take the even."

"Sounds good."

The expression on his face worried her. Dylan was dead. "Promise me you won't hurt him."

Joe glared, making no guarantee.

"Please, text me if you find him. Let me deal with him until you cool down. Gracefall needs their singer."

The elevator stopped, and the doors opened. She stepped out and turned to Joe. "Promise."

He pressed the close door button without saying a word.

Shit! She had to find Dylan before Joe.

Melody rushed down the hallway—no sign of a naked rock star. At the end of the hallway, there were another set of elevators. She was ready to step in and check another floor when the elevator across the hall dinged and opened.

"Mellie, Mel!" With his arms stretched out, a bottle of Jack Daniels in one hand, and naked as the day he was born,

Dylan hugged her. "Come." He pulled her down the hallway. "Letsssss partaaaaaaay!" he belted.

"Dylan!" She pulled away. "You can't be out here disturbing the hotel guests. Let's get you back to your room."

He stopped and eyed her up and down. He shook his finger at her. "I knew it."

"Knew what?"

He winked and staggered toward her. "It was me you wanted all along, not Joe." He stumbled, and Melody caught him.

"Dylan, you're drunk. You know I love your brother."

His demeanor changed to anger. "See, all you bitches are the same." He took a gulp from the bottle and walked down the hall.

She had to do something to stop him. She didn't want to call Joe right away. Breaking up a brotherly brawl wasn't on her bucket list.

Melody reached into her purse and pulled out a pair of pink, furry handcuffs, the ones Sal had given her in the record label's office. He'd told her to keep them handy, but when she asked why, he wouldn't tell her. Now, she knew why.

She cocked her hip to the side and twirled the fuzzy cuffs around her finger. "Dylan!"

He turned around. A big smile spread across his face. His steel-gray eyes were hauntingly familiar. *Joe.* He sauntered toward her, biting his bottom lip, looking at her like he was already picturing her naked. "Fuck yeah, Mellie!"

Melody clamped one end of the cuffs to his wrist and held onto the other end. She pulled him behind her to the elevators.

"Your ass looks amazing in that dress."

Her stomach knotted in reaction. This was Joe's brother.

She had no sexual feelings toward him whatsoever. However, she was desperate to get Dylan back to his room and avoid a night in jail. She turned on the charm, looking over her shoulder. "You should see what I have on underneath."

The elevator doors opened, and they slid in. "Can I get a sneak peek?" He closed the space between and lifted her dress. She stopped him. "Let's wait until we get into the room." She placed her hands on his chest, avoiding a kiss.

"Suit yourself, Mellie. Everyone wants to sleep with a rock star."

"Is that so?"

"Yep. When you become famous, everyone wants a piece of you. They'll even steal your girl." He leaned against the back of the elevator. "Fucking Davidson."

Melody had no idea what Dylan was talking about, but something had him upset. "Dylan, the alcohol has gone to your head."

He gave her a wicked grin. "Speaking of head."

What the...wrong word choice to use in the presence of a drunk, sexed-out rock star.

The doors opened in time for Melody to avoid another kiss.

She tugged on the cuffs, leading him down the hall. "Where's your room key?"

"I don't know. You can search me." His free arm slid around her waist. "You smell so good, Mellie."

They reached his room. His shirt and jeans were lying next to the door in a heap. "There's my clothes." Dylan picked up his jeans. As he fumbled around for the key, she texted Joe.

Melody: Found Dylan. Met me in your room.

"Found it." Dylan waved the key in front of the sensor.

"Give that to me." She took the key and swiped it. Green light. The door opened.

Dylan studied the sensor. "So that's how it works."

Melody rolled her eyes. Hadn't he ever heard of alcohol killing brain cells? It was a good thing he was pretty.

She turned to Dylan, still playing the wanton groupie. "Which bed is yours?"

He tipped his chin toward the bed next to the air conditioner. She led him to the bed, then pushed him on it. "Hell yeah, Melody Sterling likes it rough." Before she could move out of the way, he pulled her on top of him. His hands were all over her ass.

She sat up, straddling him. "Hands above your head."

"Yes, ma'am."

She clipped the other half of the cuffs to the headboard. He struggled against the restraints. "Usually, I'm the one doing the cuffing."

The hotel room door busted open. Joe strode in. "What the fuck!"

"It's not what it looks like, Joe." She climbed off Dylan.

"Yes, it is." Dylan tugged at the cuffs. "Get back here, Mellie."

She walked over to Joe, adjusting her dress. "He's drunk. He's your responsibility now." She picked up her purse and headed toward the door.

"Wait." Joe grabbed her arm. "What about dinner?" He rubbed the back of his neck. "What about tonight?"

"Tonight?" She was D.O.N.E! Here they were again, interrupted. Would she ever get Joe alone? "Little bro needs a babysitter. Make sure he doesn't choke on his vomit. We need him alive for Saturday's show."

"Mellie," Dylan begged. "Come on."

She peered over Joe's shoulder. "Sweet dreams, Dylan."

She handed Joe the key to the cuffs. "Make sure he's sober before releasing him."

"I'm sorry, Mel. This wasn't what I had in mind tonight." He held her hand. "When he passes out, how about I meet you in your room? We can continue our date."

It was over. Her perfect night with Joe was ruined. She didn't blame him. The mood was gone. Pretending to flirt with Joe's brother made her feel dirty. The whole rock star world made her feel dirty. "I'm not in the mood."

"I'm sorry." He looked dejected, and Melody knew it wasn't fair to Joe, but she'd had it.

She threw her arms in the air, frustrated. "Hey, that's rock and roll for ya." She opened the door and left without a goodnight kiss, and without Joe.

14

"Wake up, asshole." Joe kicked the mattress Dylan slept on.

"What the fuck, dude?" Dylan protested.

"We need to talk, for reals." Joe grabbed a chair from the small desk across the room. He sat it in front of his brother and straddled it. He was pissed. Instead of staying the night with Mel, he'd spent the night listening to Tyler snore and Dylan puke. "Shit's going to change."

Dylan sat up in a hungover haze. "What happened last night?"

"I don't know. You tell me."

Dylan raised his hand. The pink fuzzy handcuff dangled from his wrist. "Oh shit. Mel. We didn't...you know...did we? She was coming onto me, bro."

Joe kicked the mattress again. "No, you didn't, and she wasn't coming onto you. She was trying to save your ass from getting arrested. What were you thinking?"

"I wasn't." Dylan hung his head. "Ash is dating Davidson."

"What?"

"She called me last night to tell me she was in town for Davidson's birthday party. I asked her to go with me, but..." He scrubbed his face. "It doesn't matter. They deserve each other."

Ash was Dylan's ex, and he was still madly in love with her. Little bro was covering up an old wound that had never healed. The breakup was completely his fault. Both being lead singers in rock and roll bands, egos had gotten in the way. Dylan couldn't handle his woman quickly making a name for herself in an industry he'd spent years hustling and gigging to get to the top. Joe had watched the whole thing blow up. "Listen, I feel for you, but you can't drink yourself stupid. You're being selfish. Instead of spending the night with Mel, I had to babysit your ass."

Dylan turned his head and looked at him with a smirk. "Cock blocked again."

"Fuck you. I'm serious. I see you slipping out of control. I don't want to see you go down the same road as Karen. We worked too hard to get out of that hell. You're better than that, bro."

"What are you saying? I'm a drug addict like mom?"

"No, I just—"

"Just what? One night, I get out of control. That doesn't make me a junkie."

"It's more than last night."

"Look, I'm sorry I fucked up date night." Dylan got out of bed and headed toward the bathroom.

Joe shot out of the chair, knocking it over. He grabbed his brother's arm. "Gracefall is my life. I won't allow you to screw it up."

Heated glares met, nostrils flared, and jawlines tightened. Joe held back, for if he said what was really on his mind, Gracefall would be auditioning for a new lead singer.

Dylan pulled away. "I'm too hungover to deal with your shit. Instead of lecturing a junkie, go fuck your girlfriend." He strode into the bathroom and slammed the door.

Furious, Joe paced and rubbed the back of his neck, calming himself before he said something he'd regret.

The out-of-control drinking. The mood swings. The fact their mother was a drug addict. All the signs were there. He prayed he was wrong.

Joe stood, waiting for Dylan to come out, but it was obvious little bro had shut him out. No need to keep banging his head against the wall.

He pounded his fist on the door. "You'll apologize to Mel, understand?"

The toilet flushed in response.

"Real mature, asshole." Joe grabbed his duffle bag and stormed out of the room.

Joe headed to Mel's room. He had major damage control to settle with her. Nowhere in her job description did it say she had to babysit drunken a-holes. Their beautiful night alone had been ruined, and he'd felt responsible for the shit show.

God, he hoped she wasn't still mad at him.

$\sim$

*J*oe paced outside Melody's room as he performed a time check. *Ten a.m., she should be up.* The last thing he wanted was to wake her and make her mad. He was already in the doghouse. *Fucking Dylan.*

He rapped on the door, praying she'd let him in but understood if she didn't. Little bro's stunt last night was an example of why Mel hated the rock and roll lifestyle. She'd already lived with her dad's band. He'd been selfish to think she'd be happy living on the road with rockers. He wanted her here, but he wasn't sure she wanted to be.

To his surprise, the door opened. There was Mel, wearing a t-shirt, shorts, and bedhead, looking sexy as hell. "You know, you shouldn't open your door to strangers." He hoped she was in a joking mood.

She leaned against the doorjamb and folded her arms. "There's only one person I know who knocks to the beat of "We Will Rock You." She gave him a half-smile—it was a good start.

"Can I come in?"

She held the door open, inviting him in. This was a good sign. "How's Dylan?"

"Hungover and pissed off."

"Really?" She raised her brow at him. "He shouldn't be the one pissed off."

He completely understood her frustration. Joe rubbed the back of his neck, praying she would forgive him. "I know. There's no excuse for his behavior. You don't deserve it."

He hated the way she was glaring at him, standing with her arms crossed tightly across her chest. He got it—she was mad.

"I know you're upset. Trust me, the last thing I wanted was to spend last night without you."

"So, what happened? Why was Dylan blitzed out of his mind?"

Joe took a seat at the end of the chaise lounge and rested his forearms on his thighs as he thought about what to say. He was embarrassed by Dylan's actions, and quite frankly he never wanted to see his girlfriend straddling his brother again. "His ex called him last night. Long story short, Ash is dating Davidson. The news set Dylan off."

"What? Davidson is your manager. I knew that guy was slimy."

"Yeah, but Davidson is a genius when it comes to managing the band. He's a dick, but he makes shit happen."

She sat down next to him. "Guess I can't *totally* fault Dylan for last night. I'm sure it's going to be hard to trust the guy who stole his girl. Hopefully, we won't have a repeat tonight at the party."

Shit. He'd forgotten about Davidson's birthday bash. He'd have to keep a close eye on little bro. He wouldn't put Mel through another night of drunken stupidity. "There's more. I lost my temper with Dylan."

She looked at him with alarm. "What happened? Is Dylan still alive?"

That was a good question. Physically he was, but inside he had his doubts. "Yes. But I made things worse. I called him out on his drinking, and the conversation ended with him thinking that I think he's a junkie."

"You think he's using?"

"No." At least that's what he wanted to believe. But with Dylan it was a slippery slope. Drug users ran in the family. "I think he's drinking to escape. I don't want to see him destroy his life."

"I'm sure once he cools off, he'll realize you were trying to help."

Joe shrugged. "Yeah, you're probably right. I just feel like a real asshole."

Melody stood before him, wedged between his legs. Her hands grazed his cheeks as he looked up into the most beautiful hazel eyes. "Speaking from experience with my mom, you're going to have to let him hit rock bottom. Right now, he doesn't see drinking as a problem, and you can't tell him otherwise. He needs to be honest with himself and deal with the breakup in a healthy way."

God, he wanted to tell her the truth about his mom and the abuse, but he couldn't. He couldn't tell her that Dylan drank to numb the years of physical abuse he'd endured, and that the breakup had pushed him over the edge. He couldn't tell her that the darkest hour for the Grace brothers didn't come at night. Their monsters were real.

She gave him that magic smile that lit his soul. "You're a good man, Joe. You'll be there for Dylan when he needs you, just like you've always been there for me."

He wanted to be the man she saw, but right now he felt like a fake for lying to her all these years. Needing her comforting touch, he wrapped his arms around her waist and pulled her into a hug. "Mel, I'm always here for you."

"I know." She hugged him back, cradling his head to her chest.

He breathed her in, filling his nose with her jasmine scent. Her hands stroked his hair, his head, and his neck in the most soothing, sensual way that made him feel both loved and wanted. With Mel, the world melted away, along with his lie.

Lost in the moment, he kissed her breast through her t-shirt and was rewarded with a sigh and a hardened nipple. He continued kissing her breasts, giving each one his full attention as he slid his hands up her shirt, grazing her back.

With her sigh reassuring him he was on the right course, he moved his hands to the front, cupping both breasts and squeezing. Fuck, he loved her tits—soft and full. He lightly pinched and played with her nipples, loving the feel of them hardening more. She leaned her head back and gave him the sweetest erotic moan that went straight to his dick. He needed her naked—now.

Joe lifted her shirt over her head, tossing it on the floor. He went right back to work, kissing, licking, squeezing her beautiful fucking tits. He could sit here all day just playing her boobs, but someone else wanted in on the action. His dick went hard just seeing her naked.

As if he'd had a hard enough time keeping his dick at bay, she straddled him. He claimed her mouth with passion and a promise that tonight they were sealing the deal. There was no turning back.

He shoved his hands down her shorts and panties and squeezed her ass, pressing it against his aching cock. "Fuck, Mel, I want you."

She sat up and tugged his shirt off. She pinned him with a lustful glare. "Then take me."

Fuck yeah!

He picked her up, and she wrapped her legs around his waist, her arms around his neck. Their mouths coiled in a lustful craze they both couldn't nor wouldn't contain. He took her into the bedroom, which was separated from the living room. The French doors were open, inviting him in.

He broke the kiss, and she continued it down his neck. "Where's your phone?"

"On the nightstand. Why?"

He laid her on the king-sized bed. "Hold that thought." He walked over to the nightstand and grabbed her phone, shutting it off.

"What are you doing?"

"I'm not getting cock blocked again."

She giggled as he returned to her.

Their mouths found each other again, picking up where they had left off. Sometime between shutting her phone off and returning, she'd removed her shorts and panties and was ready for him.

As he lay down, she wrapped her legs around him, pulling him on top of her and into a kiss. He had to brace himself with his arms so he wouldn't squish her. Her touch left fiery trails down his chest as she slid her hands down his body to the waistband of his jeans. Just the thought of her touching his dick overwhelmed him—in a good way. Knowing that she wanted him was the best high ever.

She teased him, stroking him through his jeans, wrenching his need tighter and tighter. The button of his jeans popped open, and Melody's hand slid down the front. A hiss escaped him at first contact. She stroked the length of him in one fluid motion, then up again. "I need you naked." She unzipped his fly and tugged his jeans down. Shortly after freeing his dick from the jeans, her hand was back on him, sliding up and down, gripping him tight.

He reached down to touch her, and she stopped him. "Keep your hands where they are. I want to make you feel good."

"I won't stop you," he smiled at her, loving the heavy look in her eyes.

Her hand wrapped around his dick felt amazing. It was like she could read his mind, knowing when to speed up, when to grip him tighter. Lost in Melody, his body was hers do what she wanted with. He had no problem with that.

Melody trailed kisses down his neck, across his shoulder, and to his chest. She shimmied down beneath him, kissing, and licking all the way down to his stomach. Her hands had left his dick and were now on his ass, but he didn't mind, because where she was heading with her mouth made up for it.

Her hot, wet tongue licked the length of him, and he almost came undone. "Fuck, you feel good."

Her hands back on him, she moaned as she took him in her mouth, little by little, torturing him with her sweet lips. She found a rhythm that threatened to send him over the edge. Joe gripped the comforter. His arms shook from holding up his big body. His knees were grinding into the bed. Fuck it all. He'd plank here all night just to have Melody's mouth on him.

But she felt too damn good. Sucking, licking, her teeth grazing his dick. "Fuck." He reached down and pulled her up. "Come here, baby."

"You have no idea how much you turn me on." She kissed his neck.

"I have a good idea. I feel the same way."

"Then fuck me, Joe, and don't hold back. Fuck me like the woman you desire, not your childhood friend."

He grabbed his jeans, which were lying next to him, and pulled out a condom. In record time, he had the damn wrapper ripped open and was fully sheathed. He lifted her leg and rested it on his shoulder, then thrust deep inside her. He didn't mean for it to be rough, but she was so hot, wet, and ready for him.

"Joe," she moaned and wrapped her arms around his neck.

She felt so good, her warmth engulfing him, tight around his dick. He looked down between them, taking her in. Nobody was more beautiful than Melody Sterling. Everything about her turned him on, twisting him with carnal need. This was the moment they had been waiting for.

He pulled back slightly, only to thrust in deeper. He did it again and again until he found a rhythm that drove Melody crazy. She squirmed beneath him, digging her heels against his ass. He felt her walls tighten around him. "Come for me, baby," he whispered in her ear as he nuzzled her neck.

Her body quivered. "Fuck, Joe," she panted breathlessly.

Faster, harder, he rode her over the edge, and he was right there with her, exploding into bliss.

∼

*O*ut of breath, Joe collapsed next to Melody. She lay there listening to their heavy breathing. Her brain went straight to analyzing the situation. What the fuck had they done? Her body tensed as that thought looped inside her head. Everything felt right, but she couldn't shake the pact they'd made. For so long she'd suppressed her love for him. She needed a minute to process what had just happened.

"Hey."

She turned her head, facing him. "Hey."

He reached down and took her hand in his, then kissed it. "Don't do it, Mel."

"Do what?"

"I know what you're doing. You're overthinking things. There's nothing to analyze." He wrapped his arms around her, pulling her into a hug.

She laid her head on his chest, submerging into his warmth. "I can't help it."

"Just live in the moment with me." He kissed the top of her head. "Nothing else matters."

She exhaled and relaxed into his embrace. Joe was right —nothing mattered right now except living in the moment.

A comfortable silence fell over them. Being in his arms, the world faded away. She wished she could make time stand still so they could stay just like this forever. It was an ambitious wish being that Joe was a rock star. She wasn't the only one that wanted a piece of him, and that's what scared her the most.

She wrapped her arms around him tighter. "I love you, Joe Grace."

He tipped her chin up and gazed into her eyes. "I love you." He claimed her mouth, and need shot through her body. As if he'd read her mind, he pulled her on top of him. "I'm ready for round two." He wiggled his brows.

Melody stared down at him as he brushed her hair from her face. She took in his strong, chiseled jawline, his full lips, his nose ring, his beard that did fascinating things to her skin. She embraced the contentment she felt being held in his arms. Taking in everything that was Joe, she lived in the moment. "How do you know exactly what I need?"

"Because I know you better than you know yourself. Trust me, beautiful." He kissed her slowly, building up to a passionate hunger. Butterflies fluttered in her stomach as his hands slid down her body and palmed her ass.

Round two promised to be just as mind blowing as round one.

15

*A*fter spending all morning and afternoon in bed with Joe, avoiding the thought of Davidson's party, Melody had pried herself away to shower and get ready for tonight. Through the bathroom mirror as she fastened her earrings, she watched Joe fidgeting with his white button-down dress shirt.

"I don't understand why Kimmy is making us wear formal clothing at the party. I can't play drums in this shit."

Gracefall was playing at the party tonight for hundreds of Davidson's closest friends. More like closest ass kissers. She knew his kind. He was the obnoxious guy in the room, making the most noise just so he'd be seen. Yeah, tonight was going to be fun—not.

Melody smiled and walked over to Joe. "Here, let me help." She unbuttoned his shirt and took it off, leaving behind his white tank top undershirt. She untucked it from his dress pants. "There."

"Baby, we're supposed to be getting dressed, not undressed." He grabbed her around the waist and pulled her against him. "But I'm not complaining."

She placed her hands on his chest. Her eyes were drawn to the tattoos peeking out from under his shirt, remembering the Celtic cross on his right pec with her name on it. No matter what happened, she would always be Joe Grace's girl. "We have a party to attend."

He dipped his head down and claimed her lips. "I'd rather stay here with you, naked and in bed."

Looking at him dressed formally verses his normal rock tee and jeans, she liked this side of Joe. His mohawk was tamed and braided back, resting at the nape of his neck. Instead of the smell of sweat from after a show, his aftershave permeated the bathroom, turning her on. "You look good, Rock Star. Kimmy would approve of our wardrobe change."

"What would I do without you?"

"Oh, there's plenty of women who wouldn't mind being your personal stylist," she joked as she walked back to the vanity to recheck her makeup. But deep down she knew it was the truth. Women at shows threw themselves at Joe. She didn't blame them—he was sexy. She just prayed his eyes wouldn't stray from her.

"Very funny, Sterling." He slapped her ass. "We should get going. Tonight should be interesting." He walked out of the bathroom, stretching his arms, looking as if he was free again, without the shirt.

"I'll be right there."

"You look fucking sexy." He called out from the bedroom. "Come on."

"Give me a minute." She rolled her eyes. Taking one last look in the mirror, she adjusted the spaghetti straps on her dress. She didn't recognize her own reflection. Black leather dress, black stilettos, and ruby-red lips was a much different vibe from her cutoffs. The daily grind of the road showed under her eyes. There wasn't enough concealer to hide those dark circles. In the two days off from the road, she'd realized how much the whirlwind of rock and roll had sucked her in. She was tired of rushing to shows and chasing after the next one. The mayhem of after-show parties...yeah, she was done with that drunken mess.

But seeing Joe on stage, she totally got it. Their fans loved them. Gracefall was born to perform.

"Are you coming?" Joe's voice shook her free from her thoughts.

"Be right there." She stepped out of the bathroom and grabbed her purse. Joe was already at the door, holding it open as her cell went off.

The world came to a screeching halt. They looked at each other as if to say "what now?" If this was another Dylan emergency, she'd be on the next plane home.

She pulled her phone from her purse. It was a California number, but she didn't recognize the caller. "Not Dylan."

The world spun again as Joe exhaled in relief.

"I'll catch up," she told Joe.

"I'll wait outside for you."

She nodded as she answered. "Melody Sterling."

"Miss Sterling, this is Ben from the Los Angles Orchestra. How are you this evening?"

Her heart sank to the floor. *LA Orchestra?* "Um, good."

"I'm calling because we have an unexpected cellist position available in the orchestra. The committee was quite impressed with your audition."

Oh. My. God! She impressed a committee of fellow cellists. This wasn't an easy task. These men and women were at the highest level of excellence, highly decorated and accomplished musicians. She'd spent ten weeks preparing for the audition and an ungodly amount of practice time.

However, she'd gotten the dreaded rejection call; she hadn't made the cut. What had changed? "I'm sorry. You must be mistaken—"

"No mistake, Miss Sterling. We want you to come down for a week trial period with the orchestra. We think you would fit in perfectly. That is, if you're still interested."

"Yes! Of course, I am." She tried not to sound overly excited, but she couldn't help it.

"I know this is all overwhelming. Take a couple days and get back with me."

"Yes." Her head was spinning with thoughts. Her dream of playing in the LA Orchestra was coming true.

"It was good talking with you, Miss Sterling. Hope to hear from you soon."

The call ended before she could conjure up a response. She was stunned, speechless.

Reality set in. She was already committed to the tour. She couldn't let Joe down and leave. But this was her dream. Being a rock star was his.

They needed to talk, but she didn't know how to approach the subject. She had an obligation to Joe and the band. There would be other auditions. But this was an opportunity she couldn't turn down. What was she going to do? She needed to process everything before she confronted Joe. The last thing she wanted to do was drop the orchestra bomb before the birthday party. Gracefall would be playing a couple songs. Joe didn't need to deal with this now. It could wait.

"Hey," Joe knocked on the door, breaking through her thoughts. "Everything okay?"

"Yeah, I'm good." Putting her dreams aside, she put on her best game face before leaving the room. Sex, drugs, and rock and roll—that's life in the fast lane.

16

The Ripper, a nightclub in downtown Albany, was electrified tonight. The downstairs area was packed with screaming fans waiting for Gracefall to go on stage for a one-night birthday party concert for Davidson. Melody was among the chaos anticipating the show. Watching Gracefall live never got old.

The lights dimmed and were replaced by neon strobes and smoke. When the spotlight lit center stage, Dylan stood like a rock god clenching the microphone stand. "Are you ready to surrender to the unknown?" he growled into the mic, and the crowd went wild.

Melody's heart pounded along with the fast-driving beat of "Surrender to the Unknown," Gracefall's claim to fame. She couldn't take her eyes off the sexy beast behind the drum kit. She'd watched every show on the tour, and every night she'd felt the same electric wave of excitement light her body up.

Dynamite-exploding energy detonated from Dylan as he pumped up the crowd. Even the back of the room felt the shockwaves. Mox, the showoff, wailed into the guitar riff while Tyler kept the bass groove steady. The rock swagger between the two of them had the front-row girls eating from the palm of their hands. And Joe, he was the heartbeat of the song. Every beat flowed straight through you. Together, they were solid, gelled as one.

The set ended with a Gracefall version of "Happy Fucking Birthday." Mel snickered when Dylan replaced Davidson's name with *Asshole*. However, the crowd was so loud that it got drowned out. No one noticed but her. Knowing what she did about their manager and Dylan's ex, it must have killed Dylan to be here tonight. She prayed she wouldn't have to use the pink, furry handcuffs again. Ever.

As the set ended, she shouldered her way through the crowd to the stairs for the VIP section, where the private party had already started. Nervousness set in. She hated the parties.

The walls were black with lighted pieces of rock and roll art on display. A red velvet curtain hung behind a small stage, where a band played under a massive chandelier. The allure of sex set the tone in the room. As the crowded dance floor moved to the seductive beat, men and women continued switching partners and making out with whoever was willing. It looked more like an orgy instead of dancing.

This part of the rock lifestyle wasn't her scene at all.

Feeling uncomfortable, she kept her eyes down, avoiding eye contact as she walked next to the dance floor. When she reached the end, someone grabbed her arm. Whiskey wafted past her nose and turned her stomach. Startled, she looked up to a well-dressed man with dark hair. She didn't know him. "Dance with me," he demanded and pulled her toward the dancing orgy.

Melody planted her feet and pulled away. She glared at

the guy, and he moved on to another blonde who had walked by.

With her nerves shaken, she took a deep breath as she made her way to the back of the lounge. She sat down at the bar and ordered a drink to calm herself.

Where the hell was Joe?

She swiveled around, searching the crowd for him. Every booth, couch, chair, someone was getting off. She felt her cheeks blush as she saw two chicks making out in front of a long-haired, leather-clad guy. He looked famous, but she didn't recognize him.

This whole scene felt sleazy.

She turned back around and ordered another drink. The first rum and coke went down too easily.

"Melody Sterling," a deep voice yelled over the music.

She cringed. *Davidson.*

She turned around and gave him her best fake smile. "Davidson." He came in for a hug, and she ignored him and turned back to the bar, praying he wouldn't stay long. *Where was Joe?*

He sat down next her and ordered a drink. "I'm sorry we got off on the wrong foot."

The annoying smell of his cologne was on the verge of giving her a headache. "Yeah, me too," she lied. "Happy Birthday. This is some party you have here."

He swung around in his seat and leaned his back against the bar, looking out into crowd. "Yeah, I wanted to keep it small." He laughed, showing off his pearly whites.

"Right." She returned the smile and took a sip of her drink.

"So, how do you like being on tour with my boys?" he asked.

She lifted a brow. "It's a party for sure."

"You know the band doesn't get to have all the fun. You can, too." He winked.

She didn't know where Davidson was going, but something inside warned her not to let him rattle her.

He ordered her another drink, which she really didn't need. "You, too, can have anything you want. All you have to do is ask."

Her brows creased. "I'm not sure where you're going with this."

"Listen, I know you and Joe have a thing going on, and I know the music scene. Musicians like to indulge, and women are happy to oblige. If you want things to work out, you'll let him get his fix."

"You don't know Joe very well, then. He's not the cheating kind."

"He's a musician, right?"

She nodded.

"Every night on stage there's a crowd of women who what to fuck him. You can't be there all the time. He's bound to mess up. So, that's why I say you can have your fun, too. It's a win-win situation."

Anger flushed her cheeks. She couldn't believe what he was saying. Free love? What the hell? They weren't in the sixties. This exact way of thinking had destroyed her parents, had sent her mother straight to the bottle.

"Look, sweetheart, don't take it personally. It's my job to snuff out the drama and make sure the band is happy. I take care of my boys." He seductively ran his finger up and down her arm. Gooseflesh pricked her skin, as his hand was cold from holding his drink. "You're a beautiful woman. I want to make sure you're happy, too."

She pulled her arm away, feeling the sleaze of his words.

"Just like you've taken care of Dylan. I mean, you're screwing his ex, right?"

Davidson straightened in his chair. His eyes fixed in front of him as his arrogant demeanor crumbled before her. He took a long sip of his drink.

"No drama there, right?" she added.

"Ash and Dylan are toxic together. I just happened to be there when Ash needed me."

"Right, making sure YOUR BOYS are happy. Well, I've seen your efforts, and to be frank, you suck. I've known these guys for a hell of a lot longer than you. Hell, they used to practice in my father's garage. It's sleazes like you that give this industry a bad name."

"Well." He set down his empty glass. "I see I've over-stayed my welcome."

She nodded and reached for her drink. "You have."

"Let me leave you with this." He gazed into her eyes as serious as a heartbeat. "I know Joe. He'll mess up. They all do."

And there it was. The seed of doubt planted in her head.

Melody glared at him as he walked away, disappearing into the crowd. Who in the hell did he think he was? Joe would never cheat on her. They had too much history together. She grabbed the third rum and coke and brought the glass to her lips. She stopped. A vision of her mother passed out on the living room couch flashed before her. She'd tended to her mother's hang-overs too many times, all because of a broken heart. Was this how it all started? Was she following her mother's tragic past?

It couldn't be.

She set the glass down and frantically reached into her purse to take out her cell. No text from Joe.

Where are you?

~

A group of fans had stopped Joe, Moxley, and Tyler after the set. Dylan was the lucky one and had made it out alive and to the VIP lounge. He'd gloated by flipping them the finger from the balcony.

All Joe wanted was to get upstairs and find Mel. He had the perfect headache excuse to leave early so he and Mel could finally be alone and tangled in the sheets. Her ass was his tonight.

"Hey, Joe."

He turned around to a red-headed she-devil in a little black dress and stilettos. *Shit!* This wasn't good. "Hey, Ash."

"Gracefall was on point tonight. You guys sounded amazing."

"Thanks." He turned back around and signed a photo for a fan, praying she'd go away. Ash tapped him on the shoulder. Hesitantly, he faced her.

"I was wondering if you've seen Dylan." She tucked a long strand of red hair behind her ear. "I need to talk to him."

"I think it's better if you don't."

"Joe, please. If you know where he is, tell me."

Her pleading blue eyes cut right through him. "Fine, but first we need to talk."

"Fine."

"Good." First, he needed to find a place quieter than backstage. He tipped his chin to the stairs leading to the VIP lounge. He followed her upstairs, where they found a private booth. Ash scooted across the leather couch, and he followed.

"Listen, I'm going to be straight. Dylan's a wreck. When

you called and told him about Davidson, he lost his shit. My girlfriend had to cuff him to the hotel bed."

Shock washed over her face. "Seriously?"

"I don't know what you were trying to accomplish, but I suggest you leave him alone. He needs time to heal, or he's going to lose everything."

"I wasn't trying anything. I miss him, that's all." The sorrow in her voice went straight to his heart.

"Dating Davidson is a low blow, Ash. Dylan loves you."

"Dylan only loves himself." Her pale cheeks reddened. "He couldn't be happy for me when my band finally got signed. I can't compete with his ego. At least Davidson saw potential in Blushing Alice and helped us take it to the next level."

"I can't argue with that." He shook his head. Little egomaniac had some serious relationship flaws. Hell, growing up in a house of pain, he wasn't surprised.

"Joe, he left me. I never left." Her eyes watered and threatened to spill over.

Ash, on the verge of crying was an awkward situation. He didn't know what to say and didn't want to do the wrong thing. Playing it safe, he nudged her shoulder with his. "You were good for him."

"We were toxic." A small laugh escaped her. "It's better this way."

"I'm sorry, Ash." He really was. Ash was a good woman. Too good for little bro.

"It's not your fault, Grace." She smiled and sniffled, pretending all was fine. "You're one of the good guys." She wiped her cheek. "God, look at me. I'm a hot mess."

"Hey," he said softly as he lifted her chin so she would look at him. "It's okay to be a hot mess."

"No." She shook her head and pulled away, determined

to get it together. "It's time I got over Dylan. What the hell? I'm crying at a party." She straightened and wiped the running mascara from under her eyes. "I should be with Davidson instead of boohooing over my ex."

The one thing that brought him to his knees was a crying woman. "Ash. It's okay. No judgment here."

"I should go."

He slid out of the booth, and she followed. "Hey, you'll be all right, Ash." He pulled her into a hug. Even though she acted as if she didn't need comforting, her tight hold told him differently. "You're a strong woman."

"I know." She stepped out of his embrace. "Thank you, Grace." She gave him a kiss on the cheek, then walked away.

He stood there for a moment, feeling bad for Dylan and Ash, and appreciated having a woman like Mel in his life. He finally had everything he'd worked so hard for. He'd gotten himself and Dylan out of the trailer park and away from Karen, his band was at the top of their game, he was financially secure, and the best part, his best friend was now his girl. He got to share his fame and fortune with the woman he loved. Lucky bastard.

Joe patted his pockets, searching for his cell. Mel was waiting for him, and he needed to text her to find out where she was. Franticly, he searched again, then realized his cell wasn't on him. *Damn!* He must have left it in the hotel room.

He looked across the crowed room. It shouldn't be hard to find a stunningly beautiful blonde in a black leather dress.

17

*A*fter Melody's text to Joe went unanswered, she'd left the bar to find him. With her nerves shaken and her brain went into overdrive. What was it about Davidson that she allowed him to get under her skin? She didn't want to believe him, but deep down she knew he'd been right.

The masses grew, making it hard to move around. Music blared from the speakers and thumped in her chest, making it hard to breathe. As she weaved through the crowd, the strobe lights, bright as fireworks, flashed and blinded her momentarily. She'd never been claustrophobic, but with her nerves a rattled mess, she was on the edge of losing it.

"Hey, Mellie."

She turned around and was relieved to see Dylan, even if he had his arms around two chicks. He excused himself and walked over, eyeing her up and down. "You're looking hot tonight."

"Have you seen Joe?" She tried to steady her voice but failed.

"No." Concern washed over his face. "Are you okay?"

"I'm fine." She played it off, hoping he'd buy it.

He leaned in so she could hear him over the loud music. "When a woman says she's fine, she's really not. Look, if it's about last night, I'm really sorry I lost my shit. I'd never," he pointed to himself, then to her, "you know—"

"Ew!"

"Ouch." He placed his hand on his chest as if insulted. "Seriously, Mel, you don't have to crush my ego."

"Dylan, I don't have time for this. I accept your apology. I need to find Joe. Text me if you see him, okay?"

"You bet."

She shouldered past him, heading to the booths in front of the lounge. Through the bright lights and fog, she saw Joe. "Joe!" she called out, but he didn't hear her over the music. He disappeared as a group of people closed in around her. *Shit!* She continued toward the booth, then paused when she saw a red-head in Joe's arms. She didn't look familiar and was beautiful.

She had to be a fan. *Just brush it off.*

Joe will mess up.

Davidson's poisonous words surfaced, and she couldn't shake them off.

Melody stopped dead in her tracks when she watched the groupie reach up and kiss Joe, lingering longer than a quick peck. He even returned the favor.

Since when did Joe kiss fans?

A lump formed at the base of her throat as she realized she'd let her guard down—she'd fallen for the fantasy of being a rock star's girlfriend. A final confirmation that she didn't fit into Joe's life. It was as if their worlds had finally collided, knocking their dreams onto the floor.

She'd witnessed her parents deal with this exact same thing, yet she'd allowed this to happen to herself. As she stood there drowning in humiliation, she couldn't think straight with the chaos of loud music and a crowded room surrounding her. What was she going to do?

She watched the groupie saunter off into the crowd and wished she could do the same disappearing act. Instead, she squared her shoulders and marched right up to Joe.

"Hey, beautiful." He leaned in for a kiss, and she turned away.

"You promised me." Her voice cracked.

"What do you mean?"

"I dropped everything to be with you on tour. I've tried to push past my fears, and I can't anymore." Anger pulsed in her veins as she thought about the dreams she'd put on hold.

"Melody, what's going on?"

"I don't blame you. I blame myself for allowing this to happen. This is your life. It's not mine." Tears burned her eyes. She wasn't breaking down in front of him—no way. "I have to go."

She turned to walk away, and he grabbed her arm. "Don't walk away. Let's talk about this."

Talking was the last thing she wanted to do right now. She wasn't listening to empty promises anymore. She should've stuck to her guns from the beginning. She yanked her arm free and strode off toward the stairs as fast as she could.

She could hear Joe calling her name, but she didn't turn around. She needed to get out of here—now. Shouldering her way toward the exit, she tried keeping it together. Still, every push and bump from the crowd threatened her resolve. She sprinted downstairs, which hours earlier had been full of Gracefall fans.

"Melody!"

She looked back to find Joe standing on the balcony, gripping the wrought-iron railing.

"Melody!" His eyes locked onto hers as he pushed his way down the stairs.

There was nothing he could say or do to make her stay. She turned back around and ran out the door.

Cabs lined the street right outside the club. Melody looked back at The Ripper, then at a taxi. Without another thought, she climbed inside.

"Where to, pretty lady?" the driver asked as he checked the traffic before pulling out.

Before she knew what she was doing, she answered, "JFK Airport."

"That's over an hour away," he warned.

"I don't care. Just drive."

As the cab drove away, she leaned back in the seat and rested her head on the window. The coolness against her cheek did nothing to calm her. She closed her eyes, fighting back the tears and the urge to tell the cab driver to stop. If she went back to the hotel, nothing would change. She needed time alone to think. First thing in the morning, she'd call Davidson with her tail tucked and tell him to find her replacement. She wasn't looking forward to that call. She wasn't a quitter, but in this case, if she wanted to keep her friendship with Joe, she had to leave the tour. No need to make a list on that decision.

"Joe." The whisper broke her heart. Her biggest fear had come true. She may have lost her best friend, anyway.

Melody got herself together. There would be plenty of time to ugly cry on the plane. She pulled out her cell from her purse and booked a flight back to California. She didn't care that it was a red-eye—she'd be home.

After booking her flight, she texted Dani, because if she called, she'd have to explain everything. Nope, not tonight.

Melody: Hey, are you up?

The message bubble blinked for what seemed like forever.

Dani: Yeah. What's up?

Melody: I need a ride home from the airport.

Dani: What? Are you okay? Of course! What happened?

Melody: Stop freaking out! I don't want to talk about it. My flight arrives at 3 a.m.

Dani: I'll be there. Love you, Mellie.

Melody: xoxo

18

*J*oe sat behind the drum kit he'd set up in Moxley's home recording studio, trying hard to keep his head in the game. Mox had invited the band over to work on some new material before heading back on the road, which under different circumstances would have made Joe pumped to collaborate with the guys. Making music was his life. But he'd lost his rhythm. And his Melody.

One day morphed into the next as Joe went through the motions. He was confused. Mel wouldn't answer his texts or calls. She'd left him no choice, so he'd called her dad. He had to know where she was, and that she was safe. Leo had warned him to give his daughter space. Joe hated that advice but listened. It drove him mad—he didn't know why she left.

And wasn't that a kick in the balls? Mel left him.

Joe took his anger out on the skins, beating the hell out of his kit like a wild man. Why did she leave without any explanation?

Mox stopped playing, then Tyler, then Dylan. They all

turned to Joe, who didn't get the message and continued playing.

"Yo, Bam-Bam!" Mox smacked Joe's cymbal with the end of his guitar.

"What the fuck, dude!" Joe threw his arms in the air. "Why aren't we playing?"

"Oh, I don't know," Dylan shrugged. "Maybe if you could stick with one groove, we could keep up."

"I don't know what you're talking about. I'm spot on." Joe pointed his drumstick at Dylan. "Not my fault you can't keep up."

"You're spot on?" Dylan laughed sarcastically. "Last night's gig sucked big donkey balls. You were all over the place. Just ask Tyler."

"Nope." Tyler shook his head. "Don't ask me. This is between you and your brother." He pulled the bass strap over his head and leaned the instrument against his amp.

"You're chicken shit, T," Dylan said.

Tyler flipped him the finger as he left the studio.

Joe stepped out from behind the drum kit and made his way to Dylan. It was apparent little bro had something to say. "What's your problem?"

Dylan stepped up, toe to toe with Joe. "You were worried about me ruining the band when you're making us sound like shit."

"Oh, this is just like you." Joe shook his head. "You're still pouting over me calling you out about your drinking."

"And you're being a dick because your girl left you." Dylan shoved him. "Suck it up, buttercup. You thought it was sooooo easy for me to just suck it up. Well, practice what you preach, brother. Move on and get back to work."

Joe's nostrils flared. He ground his teeth, unable to say all the fucking fuck-you's at once. Before he could throw a punch, Mox stepped in, fists full of t-shirt as he held them apart. "Okay, boys, take five."

Dylan shoved Mox off. His heated eyes narrowed in on Joe as he strode toward the door. "I don't see what Mellie saw in your grumpy ass."

Joe had found his last nerve. In long, powerful strides, he charged little bro. Like a brick wall, Mox held him back. "Outside, right now!"

Mox shoved him out the back door and onto the deck. Joe paced, rubbing the tension from the back of his neck.

Mox lit a cigarette and rested his arms on the redwood railing as he looked over his lakefront property. "Are you ready to talk?" he said after taking several long drags.

Joe stopped pacing and realized what an ass he'd been. Now he understood what Dylan was going through with Ash. "I don't know what to do." He stood next to his bandmate and looked out over the lake. Rippling waves smacked against the dock in a peaceful rhythm. Where did he go wrong?

"I take it you haven't heard from Mel." Mox took another drag.

"No, she's still not talking to me. What really sucks is I don't know why."

Mox's 1830's Federal-style mansion with a separate cottage and private lake was exactly what he'd wanted to give Melody. He wasn't the jealous type, but damn, Mox had found a way to have both a relationship and a successful music career. If his best friend could make it work, why couldn't he?

"I thought having Mel on the road with me would allow her to see the kind of life I could give her." He nodded toward the white and black mansion. "I want to give her a life she's accustomed to instead of lowering herself to be with the guy from the trailer park."

"Sex, drugs, and rock and roll? Did you ever stop and think rock and roll isn't her life? Let me just throw this out there. You're still keeping your mother issues from her, aren't you?"

Joe's jaw tightened. Fuck, the truth hurt.

"She loves you. You should trust her. Tell her about your mother. She wants the truth, not the big house on the hill. Stop living the lie before you lose her."

Classic Mox, smacking him upside the head with some stone-cold reality. "I do trust her."

"Good." Mox exhaled the last drag of his cigarette, then stubbed it out on the railing.

Joe watched him pull his cell phone out from his back pocket and scroll through his contacts. "Who are you calling?"

"John, our pilot."

"Why?"

"Because you're going after our girl tonight. She deserves the truth." Mox put the cell to his ear and looked at him with a raised brow. "You're lucky John is local and loves to fly."

Joe shook his head. "I don't think it's a good idea. Her dad told me to give her some space."

"It's been two days. She's had time to think." Mox held up his hand as John answered. "Hey John, I need to ask a favor from you."

As Mox made travel arrangements, Joe couldn't think of one good reason not to go. Whatever the outcome, he needed to tell her the truth and know why she'd left. It wasn't like her to leave without saying a word. What went wrong? He couldn't lose her. She was his rock, always had been. She'd kept him from spiraling into rock and roll chaos.

"Okay, bro, you're all set." Mox slid his cell back into his pocket. "Get your ass to the chopper," he joked. "Go get our girl."

Joe didn't know what to say. No one had ever done something like this for him, ever. "Thank you," he finally choked out.

Mox tipped his chin to the door, a kind gesture telling him to get the fuck out of his house without getting all sentimental.

19

*M*elody met Dani at their favorite restaurant for drinks, despite the pouring rain. Dani had finally dragged her out of the house after numerous calls and text messages begging her to meet up. Dani was worried about her. Melody understood why, but she didn't have the desire to do anything except find solitude in chocolate ice cream. It wasn't the best way to heal her wounds, but it was a good start. Getting over Joe wasn't going to be easy when she couldn't forgive herself for falling for the rock star fantasy. She should have seen it coming.

Besides self-loathing, she was exhausted from being on the road for months. Her sleep schedule was on zombie mode.

Yet tonight, here she was, dressed, full hair and makeup, and sitting across the table from Dani. She shivered, nuzzling deep inside her denim jacket. On her way in, she'd been pelted by cold rain. It had seeped through her floral maxi dress and soaked her sandals. The coffee she ordered couldn't come soon enough.

"Have you talked to him?" Dani asked as she folded her arms on the table.

"Him who?" She casually perused the menu, knowing damn well who Dani was talking about.

"You know who," Dani said. "Don't act as if you don't care. You've spent two days in bed, and by the dark circles under your eyes, you've been crying. You don't fool me."

Melody placed the menu on the table, exhaled, and tried not to cry. "I can't."

"What do you mean you can't?"

"I can't talk to him because of the way I left. I totally had a knee-jerk reaction and left without explaining."

Dani sat back in her seat with a frown. "What happened?"

"I saw Joe with another woman." Saying it out loud hit her hard. It made it real.

"Mel, what do you mean? Was it a groupie? Because they don't count."

"I don't know. She was beautiful. They acted like they knew each other."

"Did you ask Joe about her?"

She shook her head. "I couldn't. I just left."

Dani placed her hand on Melody's. "I don't blame you one bit for leaving. Even though I would never in a million years believe Joe would ever cheat on you."

"Thanks." She gave it her best smile. "I'm not sure anymore. There are things about his past he's not telling me. It's like he has two sides. There's the funny, loving side, then there's a dark side. His mom showed up on the bus one night."

"You finally got to meet his mom?"

"Yeah, but it wasn't a happy family reunion. I saw a side

of Joe I've never seen before—pure hatred. And don't get me started on Dylan. I'm worried about him."

"Good God, Mel, you need to talk to Joe. You deserve answers."

"I'm not sure." She shook her head. "He didn't tell me for a reason. Besides, I'm not into this rock and roll lifestyle, and I would never hold Joe back from his dream. Dani," she beamed, "you should see him on stage. He was born to be a rocker."

"Talk to him." Dani shrugged. "Maybe it's not what you think."

"It's complicated. It was easier when we were just friends. Now that we've crossed that line, it hurts too much to think he'd betray me."

"Well, that's kind of the point, Mel. He is your friend and has been since you were kids. You owe him the benefit of the doubt. Friends first, right? Just hear him out. You know him well enough to know when he's lying. You told me his eyebrow arches when he is fibbing. And if it was what you saw, well then you're going to have to face the music sometime."

Melody gave Dani a perturbed glare. "Really? Face the music?"

They both broke out in laughter.

"You don't have to decide tonight," Dani said between laughs. "Let's just have a good time, just us girls."

"Sounds good to me. I'm so glad we got together. This has been eating me up these last few days. I wanted to talk to Mom, and I will, but I feel bad not understanding what she went through with Dad all those years ago." Melody felt melancholy for a moment, but then she remembered her news and her excitement grew. "Oh, I can't believe I forgot to tell you."

"Tell me what?"

"Ben from the LA Orchestra called me while I was in New York. He offered me a week trial with the orchestra."

"That's amazing, Mellie!"

"I know, right?"

"So, are you going to do it? Of course, you are. Stupid question, I know."

"Well, I haven't given him a confirmed answer yet."

"Why not! This is your dream, Mel. Go for it!"

Melody smiled. "Yeah, I should." *But what about Joe...*

Dani picked up her glass of wine. "To your dreams." Melody picked up her cup of coffee and tapped the wine glass. "To dreams."

Two hours and a greasy cheeseburger later, Melody was in her car driving back home in the pouring rain. She lost herself in thought to the rhythmic sound of the windshield wipers sliding back and forth. She'd lied to Dani—she was far from okay. In truth, she was a hot mess. Her heart was broken. She missed Joe so much it hurt. She even missed the band. Her dreams were within reach, yet too far away.

Melody thought a lot over the last few days, revisiting how everything played out over and over in her mind. Did she jump to conclusions? Good God, Joe was her friend first. Since when did she just diss him without a conversation, without calling him out on his bullshit?

She pulled into the driveway and parked. The headlights shined on a huddled mass by her front door. She strained to see who it was until the man looked at her. *Joe!* Her heart took a nosedive straight into her stomach. Excitement raced through her like a freight train roaring down the tracks. She wanted to run to him, throw her arms around his neck, and hold him tightly, to feel comfort in his embrace. She didn't have the strength to do the right thing and end it.

Melody turned off the ignition and sat in silence before she turned off the headlights. She reached for the door handle and paused. She was hurt. Joe cheated, but that wasn't the sole reason why she had to end things between them. Melody had done the one thing she promised never to do. She fell for the rock and roll fantasy. She couldn't blame him for that.

Melody leaned back in the seat. She didn't want to hear excuses. She didn't care if he was angry for the way she left. All she wanted was her best friend back.

A weight settled on her heart. This time there was no running away. It was time they faced the truth—they could never be together. And she had to know about the red-head. What did she have that Melody didn't? The answer was simple—Joe.

Melody opened the car door and stepped out into the pouring rain, making a mad dash to the porch. She shook the rain off her jacket. "Hey," she greeted Joe awkwardly. His steel-gray eyes pinned on hers, breaking another piece of her already fractured heart.

"We need to talk." His voice was low and grim.

She nodded, then opened the door and let him in.

Avoiding eye contact, she took off her wet jacket. "I'll get you a towel."

She returned with two towels, giving Joe one. Drying her hair, she made her way into the kitchen. "Want a beer?"

"Got anything stronger?"

"Whiskey?"

"That'll do."

She grabbed two crystal tumblers from the overhead cabinet, placed them on the table, and poured them each a finger before handing one to Joe. As she took a sip, she stayed behind the counter, keeping distance between them.

She watched him toss back the glass and gulp it down like it was water. "Thirsty?"

His face scrunched as the whiskey burned going down. "Nah, liquid courage."

An uncomfortable silence settled between them. The question of the night—"Who's the gorgeous red-head?"— begged to be answered.

"Why did you leave, Mel?" The grave expression on his face melted her into a sappy puddle. If she would listen to her heart, she'd forgive herself and forget about the red-head.

You fell for the lie, Mel.

She swirled the whiskey as she gazed into the glass. She didn't know where to start, the groupie or his mother. Or maybe she should go straight for the throat and give him the "it's not you, it's me" answer.

"I feel like I don't know you anymore. I'm trying to understand your past, but you won't let me in. You won't let me ask questions about your mom. The night she showed up on the bus, I saw your dark side, and to be honest, it scared me. I wish you would trust me."

Joe gripped the countertop edge. "It's not about trust. I have my reasons for keeping my past a secret."

"So, I'm supposed to be okay with it all? Even the red-head I saw you with at the party?"

He snapped his head up. Confusion washed over his face as he recalled that night. "Ash? You left because of Ash?"

She crossed her arms, irritated over his reaction. "That was Ash?" She had never met her.

"Yeah, she's Dylan's ex-girlfriend. She was looking for him, and I had to talk her out of it. I didn't want a repeat of Dylan going off the deep end."

Melody felt horrible for accusing Joe of cheating, but worse, she'd allowed Davidson to put those ideas in her head. "I'm so sorry." She shook her head. "I feel like such a jerk."

"I wish you would've come to me."

"Joe, I totally had a knee-jerk reaction. Right before I saw the two of you, I had a conversation with Davidson. He brought a lot of insecurities of mine to the surface. I totally don't blame you. I blame myself."

"For what?"

Did he really not know? "Like a fool, I believed we could ignore the world around us and be together." She shook her head. "I was wrong."

"Mel." He took her hands in his. "Baby, don't say that." His voice cracked, and she almost lost it. "We can make it work. There's no one in the world that I want to share my life with more than you."

She looked up at him. "Then why don't you trust me? Tell me why you hate your mother." Her stomach knotted as she took a step back. "I need to know."

Joe stiffened. "I don't understand why it matters. I'm not cheating. I want to share my life with you. Why can't that be enough?"

"Because I need to trust you, and you need to trust me, even with your darkest secrets."

"Fuck." He shoved his hand through his mohawk.

"Tell me, or all of this is for naught. We need trust to make this work."

Melody prayed she hadn't pushed him too hard. She hated giving him an ultimatum, but she'd laid it all on the line. She deserved that much in return.

Joe left her and went into the kitchen, returning shortly with the whiskey bottle. He leaned against the counter next to her and tossed back the bottle, wiping his mouth when he was done. "I lied to you."

~

*J*oe was losing her. If he didn't start confessing, Mel would throw him out on his ass. Hell, after the truth came out about his childhood, he expected to be kicked out of her life for good.

He took in a deep breath, preparing for the difficult task. He'd blocked those hellish days from his memory. The only family that mattered were Mel's father and the band. If it wasn't for Leo Sterling, he'd be in prison.

"Mel, my mom isn't a traveling nurse. She's a crack whore. Dylan and I grew up in a trailer park, dirty and poor. I never knew my dad. Her boyfriends were drug dealers or users. As they did their drugs, no one cared that there were two children in the house. Many nights we went hungry. It was up to me to take care of Dylan. I tried to protect him." Joe paused, pushing down the rage he felt every time he went down memory nightmare lane. "I came home one night from a lesson with your dad. I was thirteen. *The Jerry Springer Show* was blaring from the living room as I walked into the kitchen and found my mom huddled in the corner, bloody and bruised. Her boyfriend had beat the shit out of her. The first thing I thought was 'Where's Dylan?' A bad feeling came over me. I ran past the bastard passed out on the recliner to our bedroom—he wasn't there. I finally found him in the bathroom, curled into a ball and shaking in the tub. He'd been beaten severely. I lost it. I grabbed the baseball bat from under my bed and strode into the living room. I don't remember how many times I hit him, but I sent the dude to the hospital.

That night, I promised Dylan I would get us out of that hellhole."

"Joe, I'm so sorry."

Sorrow filled her big, beautiful eyes, something he despised more than the idea of her knowing everything. "I don't want your pity." He didn't want it then, or now. Nor did he want her to treat him differently. Her reaction, right now, was the reason he never told her about his mom. It was ugly and dark. Back then, she was his light through the darkness. "If it wasn't for your dad, Dylan and I would have ended up in Child Protective Services."

"What do you mean?"

"I didn't know what to do, so I called your dad. I was scared. Shit, I had almost killed the guy. I had no idea if I was going to juvie or prison. He came down to the police station, and the last thing I remember was being in your dad's car driving to his place. He took us in."

"Wait. You and Dylan were living with my dad right under my nose, and I didn't know about it?"

"Your dad wanted to help. He lawyered up, wiped my record clean. He'd set up a room in the mansion for us, but I refused. I didn't want handouts, and I was too embarrassed to tell you. So, Leo converted the maintenance shed into a studio apartment for me and Dylan. He put me to work, and I paid my own way and all the court costs. Pride was the only thing I had left. I didn't want you to know about that part of my life. Hell, I wanted to forget it completely. I made your dad promise not to tell anyone, especially you."

"Wow, how did I not know?" She leaned against the counter in shock. "I just thought you were really into your lessons."

"How many trips would the daughter of the God of Thunder make to the maintenance shed?"

Melody stood speechless. The expression had gone cold on her face. Had he said too much? Was this the big breakup? God, he wished he could read her mind.

"Joe, I'm so embarrassed. I never wanted you to feel that you couldn't talk to me."

"I could talk to you, just not about that night or about Karen. I was really into you." He rubbed his thumb over her hand. "Your friendship has gotten me through some tough shit. You and Dylan were my inspiration for putting together a band so we could get the hell out of the trailer park. I wanted to make something of myself—make a future for us. Do you remember when we were kids, and we spent the summer on tour with your dad?"

She looked up at him. The brightest smile spread across her lips. "The best summer of my life."

"That summer, I was your dad's roadie. That's how I bought my first drum kit."

She shook her head. "Leo Sterling."

"Don't be mad at him."

"I'm not." Her lips lifted into a smile. "He kept his promise. I mean, he's an amazing man. I wouldn't expect anything less. He puts up with my mother from afar. He saw something special in you. I saw something special in you." She caressed his cheek. "I wish you would have told me."

He turned into her hand and kissed her palm. "Are you mad?"

"I'm not. I'm glad my dad was there for you. It really doesn't matter if I knew or not, because it wouldn't have changed a thing. I love all of you, Joe Grace." She wrapped her arms around him, and he pulled her in, hugging her tighter. It felt good to come clean. Though they'd had this thing, this draw, this togetherness all of their lives, he'd never felt unconditional love before now. She loved him—all of him.

She pushed up onto her toes and gave him a tender kiss. "I know this was hard. Thank you for telling me."

Words lodged in his throat. He couldn't express what he was feeling right now. One day it would all come out in a song, but for now he lived in the moment. He nodded, gazing down at their joined hands. "I've missed you."

"I've missed you, too."

He looked into her eyes. "All I thought about was you." He brushed back the hair that had fallen over her shoulder.

"So, does this count as a fight?" She gave him a flirtatious grin.

His brows pinched together. "A fight?"

She traced the tattoos on his arm, giving him goose-bumps and heating his flesh at the same time. "I mean, if not, that's okay. But I've heard make-up sex is pretty amazing."

"Well, then this was definitely a fight." He gazed down at her, locking in on her breasts while he ran his finger under the V-shaped neckline of her dress, teasing her skin.

She slid her hands over his chest and up to his neck, stopping midway up the back of his head where she seductively caressed his mohawk ponytail. "Have you ever had make-up sex?"

How was he supposed to answer that when her hands were sweetly torturing him? "Nothing worth talking about." He did and didn't want to ask her the same question. Firstly, he didn't want to hear about the other men in her life. They didn't count—she was with him now. Secondly, he didn't want to talk anymore—he wanted to be buried deep inside Mel. "How about you?"

She shrugged.

"Let me guess, Drew the Douchebag."

"Joe," she playfully shoved him. "That's not nice."

He laughed. "That guy couldn't satisfy himself, let alone a woman."

"Sounds like someone is jealous," she teased.

"Nah, baby, I'm not jealous." He held her chin up and kissed her deeply. "You've always been mine," he whispered against her lips.

She stepped out of his embrace. Her lust-filled eyes fixated on his as she slowly untied the front of her dress. It slid off her shoulders and fell at her feet. He took her in for a moment, gazing over her smoking-hot body, imagining all the things he would do to her.

"Come here, Rock Star." She grabbed his t-shirt and planted a hot, passionate kiss on his lips, which quickly escalated into a hungered need he'd never seen from her before. He took her in, matching her tongue for tongue. She devoured him yet at the same time totally surrendered to him.

He came up for air. "Where's your cell phone?" he asked, short of breath.

"It's on the counter behind you. What is your obsession with my phone?" She continued kissing down his neck.

Without breaking their embrace, he reached behind him and grabbed her cell. "I'm holding a grudge. I haven't forgiven it from cock blocking me."

Melody laughed.

He turned the cell off and tossed it on the counter, then turned his full attention on her. Joe lifted her up, and Melody wrapped her legs around his waist, continuing the kiss where they had left off. He grabbed her ass, slipping his hands inside her panties. Hot, wet heat woke his inner dickbrain. "Fuck, Mel, I need to be inside you."

～

*M*elody's ass hit the top of the dining room table. She'd guessed the bedroom was too far away. "So, this is happening right here on my table?" She really didn't care where, as long as he was fucking her.

She heard a rip and off her underwear went. "Fuck yeah, it is." His wicked smile sent a wanting eagerness racing straight between her legs, like she could want him more than she already did.

She fought Joe's t-shirt as she tried to desperately tug it off his big body. She needed to feel his skin on hers—now. "Are we going for a three-course meal, or are we going straight to dessert?"

"I always eat dessert first." He winked, then pulled her bra down, exposing her breasts. Her breath hitched as the cool air hit her skin and enhanced her arousal. She lay back, giving him a full-access pass. His tongue swirled over her nipple and she came undone, shoving her hands in his hair, guiding him down her body. She wanted his mouth all over her.

He trailed kisses down her stomach as he ran his fingertips along the inside of her knees, spreading her legs, then back down to her ankles, lifting and resting them over his shoulders. A shiver shot straight up her spine as his tongue licked her sensitive flesh. Concentrating at the center of her pleasure, he sucked her, licked her, pushed her toward a beautiful release. "Fuck, I love dessert," she moaned.

"Mmm." The vibration of his voice added to the pleasure, causing a sweet moan to escape her mouth. Melody arched her back, surrendering to this intimate moment. Joe was the only one who made her feel alive, beautiful, and fucking out of control.

Melody's body was no longer her own—it quivered and shook. She'd never come so hard in her life. "Joe," she panted. "Fuck me."

He unbuttoned his fly. Desire shot straight to her core. Melody sat up, and Joe wrapped her legs around him. Never had she wanted someone as much as she wanted him right now.

Heat raced through her as he pressed his tattooed body against hers. In one thrust, Joe was buried deep. By God, the way he filled her felt so good.

Needing to feel every hot muscle against her skin, she hugged him tight. It took all she had to keep the fast pace and rhythm he'd set. Every hungry thrust pushed her closer to shattering all over again, and she loved every minute of it.

Melody shuddered as she was on the brink of another orgasm. Joe held her tight, and his body stiffened. He groaned into her hair as he pulled out. Thank God he did in time. Taken over by passion, she wasn't thinking clearly. Neither of them was ready for the responsibility of a child.

They held each other tight. The sound of their breathing filled the room. She leaned back, taking in the cool air pumping through the AC vent above them.

Regaining his strength, Joe started to move then stopped. He looked at the floor. "Shit, I really liked that t-shirt."

Not understanding, she leaned forward and looked at the floor. His tee had taken one for the team. She hopped down from the table. "I'm glad one of us was thinking straight."

His big arms wrapped around her. She loved it when he held her. It made her feel protected and adored. "Yeah, that was a close one."

"Maybe we should take this party into the bedroom where the condoms are," she winked.

"After you, milady," he gestured to her bedroom.

The burning desire in his eyes rekindled her own. Excitement coursed through her—he wasn't through with her yet.

20

*M*elody's new favorite thing...make-up sex. Throughout the night and early morning, they'd had sex on the dresser, up against the wall, in the shower, and a couple hours ago, in bed.

A warm glow filled her bedroom from the morning sun shining through her window. She marveled at Joe as he slept peacefully. She had a newfound respect for him. Melody couldn't imagine a child going through what he had. She caressed his cheek. *So strong and handsome*, she mused as her fingers brushed over his beard. Joe refused to surrender to the ugliness of the world. Instead, he'd fought against it while protecting her from the truth. She couldn't fault him for that.

Meldoy scooted closer, needing to feel his warmth. She traced the black and gray skull tattoo on his right pectoral. She'd felt like such a fool for believing he'd cheated but relieved she was still his one and only. However, they were playing with fire.

Grim reality knotted in her stomach. Joe would leave her; he had a tour to finish. She wasn't going with him.

The LA Orchestra was a once-in-a-lifetime opportunity she couldn't let go. She had to tell him she was leaving the tour, which reminded her, she still needed to call Davidson. How were they going to make their relationship work? Long-distance relationships never lasted. Rock and roll was his dream, and she was proud of all his accomplishments. Could she fit in his world? Could he survive in hers?

Strong arms wrapped around her. She closed her eyes and melted into a hard, muscled body.

"Morning, beautiful," he said softly against her ear before kissing her shoulder. His voice was deep and raspy from sleep.

"Morning." She caressed his cheek as she gazed into his steel-gray eyes. The dark cloud of their future loomed over them.

"What's on your mind?" He tightened his grip around her as if he knew she needed comforting.

"How are we going to make this work?" She intentionally left out the part about the orchestra calling.

"Do you love me, Mel?"

"Of course, I do."

"Then, we'll make it work. I want to share my life with you. I have ever since I met you. If privacy is an issue, I'll request a separate tour bus for us. You don't have to manage the tour. We'll hire someone else. I just want you with me."

She shook her head. "Being in love with a musician isn't easy. I've seen this lifestyle destroy my parents. I don't want that to happen to us."

"We're not your parents."

She snapped her gaze to his.

"If you asked me to leave the band and stay here with you, I'd do it. You are my everything." He caressed her cheek. "You're all I want."

"Joe, I'd never ask you to leave the band. Seeing you on stage, there's no doubt this is your calling."

"Whew." He rolled over. "I'm glad you didn't ask me to leave. I mean...I would, but..."

She playfully shoved his arm. "I know you didn't mean it."

They laughed as she lay next to him. She stared up at the ceiling, the dark cloud still hovering. She had to tell him she wasn't going back on the road.

He turned his head toward her. Their gazes met. "Baby, we can have it all."

Melody forced a smile and felt like a coward. She couldn't tell him. Couldn't break his heart.

His cell rang from the nightstand, giving her the perfect excuse to gather her thoughts.

As Joe answered the call, Melody whispered, "Coffee?"

He nodded and kissed her.

Melody climbed out of bed and put on her robe. She padded across the bedroom floor, making her way to the kitchen. Her entire body pleasantly ached, reminding her of every place Joe had been. She smiled, remembering the pleasure as she made a pot of coffee.

Joe was her best friend. Being lovers should make her feel weird, but it didn't. This was where they should be, like everything had been heading to this point where they could be together. Everything seemed right, as if this was their time to explore this part of their relationship. All along, Joe held her heart. He deserved to know her plans. They loved each other. They could work this out.

Convinced by her pep talk, she poured two cups of coffee. She grabbed the cups and started to leave the kitchen when Joe walked out of the bedroom. She froze.

"Joe, what's wrong?"

Melody watched as he stumbled to the kitchen island, flinching when he slammed his hands on the granite countertop and hung his head. "I can't believe it."

"What?" she rushed to his side. "What happened?"

He shook his head.

Dread washed over her. "Joe, you're scaring me. Tell me what's wrong."

He slowly turned his head toward her. His grim expression was like a knife to her heart. "Mox is dead."

Numbness infused her body. Mox couldn't be dead. "What happened?"

"Bus accident." Tears filled his eyes as he looked away.

Her throat thickened with sobs. "Not Moxley."

Joe scrubbed a hand down his face. He was desperately trying to keep it all together, but she knew inside Joe was shaken to the core. "Dylan said he, Tyler, and Mox were on the bus heading to Florida for our next show. The bus was hit by a truck on the highway and lost control. Mox was thrown from the bus."

Melody's hand flew to her mouth, stifling a cry.

"Dylan has a fractured hand, and Tyler has a small head injury." He shook his head. "Fuck, Mel, I should have been on the bus."

Seeing Joe like this tore her up inside, but she needed to be strong for him—he needed her. "Hey." She wrapped her arms around him, resting her head against his chest. "It wouldn't have changed a thing."

He held her tight, gripping her robe. "I can't believe he's gone." He buried his head against her neck, his tears soaking her skin. She could feel the anger in his touch and hear the sadness in his words. "This is so unfair."

"I know, baby. I can't imagine what Sam is going through right now."

"Christ, his daughter just lost her dad."

"What can I do to help?"

"Don't let me go."

They stood there for what seemed like hours, holding onto each other for support. What happened was tragic, horrifying, and all Melody could think of was that it could've been Joe.

That was surreal. She knew her answer now. What their future would be was clear, and she couldn't be more sure.

She held him tighter. "I'm not going anywhere."

21

*J*oe stood on the back deck of Mox's house, escaping his friend's family and friends. Sam had invited everyone back to her home to celebrate Mox's life, and the place was packed.

Celebrate? Joe didn't really get the concept. He'd barely made it through the funeral, and he wasn't doing much better after the service. If another person offered their condolences, he'd lose it. Anger didn't begin to express how he was feeling. It hurt like hell.

He leaned against the railing, staring into the dark waters of the lake. Life had taken a major nosedive. A week ago, he'd been standing here with Mox, talking about the future and making music. Now, he mourned his friend. He'd never see Mox again.

For the past week, he'd been on an emotional rollercoaster of mental overload. One minute, denial would set in as he waited for Mox to call—a lie he held onto to reassure himself that everything would be normal again. Knowing there was a new normal on the horizon, anger crept in. Life was a bitch. Mox was gone too soon. He had a wife and daughter to live for. The thought of the band going on without Mox enraged him. Gracefall wasn't Gracefall without their fierce guitar genius.

Thank God Mel kept him from derailing into chaos.

The door opened behind him. Dylan walked out and stood next to him. "Hey," he said in a somber tone.

Joe nodded and took a sip of the whiskey in his glass.

"Listen, I'm not good at apologies, so I'll come out and say it. I'm a dick."

He faced his brother with a cocked brow.

"I know. I've said things out of anger. I'm sorry. All this shit going on has me thinking how lucky I am to have a big bro like you. You're all I have. I don't want to lose you."

Joe pulled his brother into a hug. "I'm not going anywhere. We'll find a way to get through this shit."

"Yep, we always do."

The door opened again. Tyler walked out, holding three full shot glasses. "Sorry to break up the family reunion." He handed Joe and Dylan a shot. "Here's to Moxley, the best fucking guitar player in the world."

"Fuck yeah," Dylan choked out and clinked his glass with Tyler's.

Joe nodded and joined in.

Tyler reached behind him and pulled a bottle of whiskey from the waistband of his pants. He poured them all another round.

Dylan held up his index finger, signaling he was next. "Here's to the man, the legend with a heart of gold."

"Cheers," Tyler and Joe said in unison, then downed their shots.

Tyler replenished the glasses again.

"Here's to the best friend a man could have." Joe was surprised he got the words past the lump in this throat.

"Man, I'm going to miss that motherfucker." Tyler leaned against the railing, folding his arms against his chest. Tyler was the outgoing one—adventure always twinkling in his eyes. His opinions were raw and rough, holding nothing back. Yet, Joe sensed he was holding back now. They all were. No one wanted to discuss the future of Gracefall without Mox.

"He was one-of-a-kind." Joe noticed how much easier it became to speak as he talked to his boys, because they were family. His family. The family he'd never had but always wanted. Mox was every bit the brother Dylan was. They all were his brothers now.

Dylan exhaled heavily. "Fuck you both."

Joe and Tyler snapped their attention on Dylan.

"Mox would be so pissed off right now. We're acting like a bunch of pussies. He'd want us to move on and kick ass. Instead, we're standing here with our dicks in the dirt, refusing to talk about the future of Gracefall."

"I don't see how Gracefall can continue," Joe said a little perturbed.

"Dylan does have a point," Tyler said. "Mox would want us to continue."

Joe crossed his arms across his chest, feeling outnumbered. "It doesn't feel right. We shouldn't even be talking about this. Not now."

"Bro, Gracefall is exploding right now," Dylan said, "If we don't continue, we'll lose our momentum. We have to find a replacement and get back on the road."

Tensions were high. Tyler poured them another shot. "We're not the first band this has happened to. If Metallica can do it, so can we."

Dylan added, "Bro, if it were me being buried, I'd sure as fuck want you to continue with this thing. Man, we didn't come this far to only go this far, and if you dudes dropped the ball and let Gracefall die, I'd haunt you with my pitchfork."

Dylan always could lighten up the room with his stupid talk, but maybe he had a point. It just seemed too early to even think about it, but Tyler was right about the momentum.

Tyler continued, "Let's talk to management about holding an audition. We'll pick the one we can stand to be around and finish the tour."

"And just like that, things will fall into place." Joe shook his head. "I can't believe this." He clenched his jaw, avoiding blowing up. How could his bandmates act as if Mox was so easily replaced? They needed time to mourn.

Dylan approached his brother and placed his hand on his shoulder. "We have to do what's best for Gracefall. You know Mox would want that...any of us would want that."

"Yeah, we can't throw it all away," Tyler added.

Joe didn't have the energy to argue. He wanted to get back inside to Mel and forget about this conversation. He'd just buried his friend, and now his bandmates were ready to replace Mox like he'd meant nothing to them. Maybe that wasn't fair, but no family was that easily replaced. Mox was the glue that kept the band together. Without him, Gracefall wasn't Gracefall. "Looks as if I'm outnumbered." He yanked the door open, and Dylan stopped him.

"Don't make us look for your replacement, too," Dylan challenged.

Joe snapped his head up. What was that supposed to mean? Because he didn't agree with them, *he* was going to be replaced?

"I see it, bro. I know what you're thinking."

"You have no clue, Dylan."

"You're thinking replacing Mox means you're being disloyal to him."

Joe was taken off guard by his brother's words. Dylan was right. Every time he thought about Gracefall moving on without Mox he felt sick to his stomach. It just didn't feel right.

"Don't quit the band because of Mox." Dylan placed his hand on his hips. "He wouldn't want that."

"Stop." Tyler stepped between the brothers. "No one is going anywhere. Emotions are high, I get it. We're brothers, and we'll get through this together. Joe, Mox will never be replaced. Dylan, Gracefall will move on. Mox would want it this way."

This was bullshit. He was in no mood to deal with business. He looked at Dylan, then to Tyler. He'd been through a lot with these guys, but could they get through Mox's death?

"Are we good?" Tyler asked. Dylan nodded, but Joe was far from good.

"I'm heading inside," Joe said. "You know where to find me." He left his bandmates and went inside. He couldn't talk about Mox or Gracefall anymore. Talking made the tragedy all too real. He wanted to forget.

Joe made his way into the living room where Mel stood next to the fireplace, holding Mox's daughter. For the first time today, he smiled.

He walked up behind her and wrapped his arms around her waist. "You want one of these?" He rested his chin on her shoulder as he watched the baby sleeping in her arms.

She giggled. "Not any time soon. Gracie is adorable, though."

A lump formed in his throat. Mox had named his

daughter after the band. Of course, he did. Mox believed in Gracefall as much as he did. *Son of bitch!* The guys were right—Gracefall had to continue for Moxley. Feeling as if Mox was looking down on him right now, Joe looked up and smiled. *Motherfucker.*

He tightened his arms around Melody, blessed to have her in his life. "Yeah, they kind of suck you in with all their cuteness, don't they?"

"Joe, she's not a kitten."

"Worse. Kittens turn into cats from Hell. Infants turn into sassy teenagers. Pick your poison."

She turned and faced him. "When the time is right, I choose a beautiful baby that looks just like his father." She kissed his cheek.

Joe faked a smile, and she saw right through it. "Hey, are you okay?"

He shrugged as he shoved his hands in the front pockets of his slacks.

"You want to get out of here? We can go for a drive."

Yes, he wanted to get out of here and go back in time. He would've kept the band off the bus. Mox would be alive. However, they didn't live in a world with that kind of magic. The magic he did have was with Mel. He'd felt the warmness and understanding of her heart. During his weakest moments, she'd held him up. Without her...he didn't want to think about a world without her. "I promised Sam I'd stick around and help clean up."

Her smile brightened his mood. "You're a good man, Joe Grace." On tiptoes, she reached up and kissed him. "I love you."

"Is she being a good girl?" Sam walked up to Mel, goggling over her daughter.

"She is," Melody beamed.

"Do you mind if I steal Joe for a second?" she asked.

"Not at all. Gracie and I will go find Dylan and Tyler."

He watched Mel walk out of the room. How in the hell did he get so lucky?

"You guys look really happy," Sam said. "It's about time y'all finally got together."

"Yeah, we are." He looked at Sam, and his heart broke. Her eyes were puffy from crying. She looked as if she hadn't slept in days. Not only was she grieving for her husband, but she was also taking care of a baby all on her own. "How are you holding up?"

She shrugged. "I miss him."

"Yeah, me too."

"Listen," Sam said. "The night before the accident, Mox and I were talking about who we wanted Gracie's godparents to be. We both agreed it should be Melody and you."

As if his heart could handle any more surprises, Joe stood speechless. Godparents? This was huge. First, Mox named his kid after the band, and now he wanted him to look after Gracie? Joe Grace responsible for another human being?

He exhaled heavily and looked at Sam, making sure she was of sound mind. This was a huge responsibility. "I'm honored. I don't know what to say."

"Say yes."

"Yes." Joy filled his heart to the point he felt like it would explode. "I mean, I'll talk to Mel about it, but yeah."

"I know life is crazy. You on tour and Mel playing in the orchestra—"

"Wait, what?" Confused, he couldn't follow what Sam was talking about. "Mel hasn't mentioned anything about the orchestra."

Devastated, Sam gasped. "I'm so sorry. I ruined the surprise. I thought she'd told you."

Something was telling him there was no surprise. Mel intentionally didn't tell him. But why? They didn't keep secrets anymore. "I'll make sure I act surprised when she tells me." He reassured Sam no harm was done.

Crying interrupted their conversation as Mel returned with a red-faced, wailing baby. "I think Gracie is hungry." She handed Sam her daughter. "Sorry, I can't help out in that department."

"Thanks, Mel. She's always hungry." Sam gave Joe a knowing look. "Think about it, okay."

"Will do." He kissed Sam's cheek, and she left.

"Think about what?" Mel asked.

"Sam and Mox want us to be godparents to Gracie, but now I'm having second thoughts." He watched her face turn from excitement to mass confusion.

"Second thoughts? What are you talking about?"

"Mel, we need to talk."

"Okay," she said hesitantly and followed him to the bedroom they were staying in.

Joe shut the door behind them. He cut right to the chase. "When were you going to tell me?"

"Tell you what?"

"The orchestra. Ring a bell?"

She gazed at the floor. "I was waiting for the right opportunity to tell you."

"So, tell me now, Mel. Tell me how you were going to leave me again without saying a word." He didn't mean to snap, but he couldn't hold back. She was leaving him...again.

She shook her head. "It's not like that."

"You can tell Sam, but not me?"

"Calm down. I'm not going anywhere. Let me explain."

He waited.

"When we were in New York, I received a call from the LA Orchestra. They offered me a one-week trial audition with the opportunity of a permanent position in the fall."

His tone changed. "Baby, that's fantastic. You should have told me sooner."

"I wasn't sure what to do. I had obligations to the band."

"Yeah, but this is your dream."

"I know, but life has changed, Joe. I can't leave you when you need me the most." She wrapped her arms around his waist. "I choose you. There'll be other auditions. The timing is all wrong. You need me, and I need you, too, right now."

He kissed the top of her head. Mel had a good heart. He couldn't allow her to sacrifice her dream because of him. "Baby, you have to take the offer. I won't let you throw it all away because of me." What was he saying? Selfishly, he didn't want to let her go, but he would regret it forever if he didn't. Playing cello in the LA Orchestra was her dream. She deserved the shot.

"Joe, you lost Mox. I don't mind going back on tour with you. You shouldn't be alone."

"Mel, my life is upside down. It's not fair to you to drag you along."

She shook her head. "Please, don't shut me out."

"I'm not." For once in his life, he'd opened the door and seen things clearly. He couldn't protect Dylan from Karen's abusive boyfriends, and he couldn't protect Mox from the accident, but he could protect Melody's happiness. She might not see it now, but she would. "Baby." He rubbed her arms. "I love you. You're catching the next flight to Cali.

You're going to your audition trial, and you're going kick ass. Live your dream."

"What about us?" Her voice cracked.

He cupped her face. "Will you wait for me?"

"Of course, I'll be here."

"Good." He smiled. "I'll see you after the tour."

22

*A*lone, Melody got off the plane at LAX, pulling a small carry-on behind her. The six-and-a-half-hour flight had been long, giving her too much time to miss Joe. He'd stayed in New York with Dylan and Tyler to help Sam finalize a few of Mox's affairs. She couldn't imagine what Joe and the guys were going through. Guilt washed over her— she should be with Joe.

Melody exited the airport and grabbed her cab, thankful the driver wasn't late. It was past midnight, and she was exhausted. She couldn't wait to get home and crawl into bed. She'd taken the latest flight out of New York so she could spend time with Joe. They had spent all morning and afternoon in bed loving each other. She didn't want to let him go. Deep down, she knew when she left that things would be different between them. Good or bad, she didn't know.

She wanted to believe Joe when he said they could have it all—she hated doubting him, but the thought of their love burning out nagged her. Losing her best friend would be devastating.

Lost in her thoughts, she closed her eyes. When she opened them again, the driver was pulling up to her house. He popped the trunk, retrieving her suitcase as she got out of the car. She paid and tipped the guy, then headed to the front door.

Like a zombie, she went through the motions of her nighttime routine, washing her face, brushing her teeth. On her way to the dresser, she saw Joe's Metallica concert tee on the bed. She brought the shirt to her nose and breathed in. Oh yeah, it still smelled like Joe, fresh and clean. She undressed and put Joe's shirt on, then crawled into bed. The sheets still smelled like him, too. She grabbed the pillow he'd slept on and hugged it. She missed him like crazy.

Melody reached over and took her cell from the nightstand. On her favorites list, she FaceTimed Joe. As she waited for him to answer, she lay back in bed and finger-brushed her hair. She had no makeup on, but she could still look sexy.

"Hey, beautiful." Joe's face filled her screen.

"Hey, Rock Star." She beamed. "I made it home. Wish you were here to tuck me in."

"Me too. How was your flight?"

"Long and exhausting."

"I see you found the shirt I left you."

She zoomed out, showing Joe the tee.

"What are you wearing under your shirt?" He wiggled his brows.

"Wouldn't you like to know?" She winked.

"I would. I haven't showered today. I can still smell you on my skin. It's driving me crazy."

"Yeah, my bedsheets smell like you. That's why I called. I needed to see your face." She rolled over on her stomach. "I miss you."

"I know, but we can do this. When does your trial audition start?"

"Tomorrow, late morning."

"You should get some rest. I'll call you tomorrow."

Casually, she pulled up her t-shirt, positioning the phone so he could see her butt cheek in the background. "I know you're more of a tits man. My ass will have to do."

"You're a tease." He smiled.

"Sweet dreams, Rock Star." She blew him a kiss, then ended the call.

23

Gracefall's new tour bus pulled into the Alabama venue in time for the guys to head to soundcheck. The stage crew and roadies had gotten there two days before, which was a good thing—the show was tonight. This was the first gig without Mox. The mood on the bus didn't have the same excitement it once did. No one knew who was replacing Mox or if the replacement was permanent or a hired gun to fill in until they found their guy or girl. Davidson wanted them back on the road—no questions asked. Management would take care of the rest.

He didn't like it. Gracefall should be in control of replacing Mox. They were the ones who had to live with the newbie for the next two months of the tour, not Davidson. The band was a tight family unit. Outsiders weren't welcome. Joe hadn't worked his ass off all these years to have someone come in and ruin everything.

Joe stretched as he got off the bus, hungover from the night before. He was not looking forward to today's announcement. It had been two weeks since Mox's death. The emotional wounds were still as fresh as the day he'd received the tragic news. The band was holding on by a thread. Dylan drank and fucked himself numb, Tyler never talked about it, and as for Joe, he was somewhere in between anger and numbness. He'd been drinking way too much. If only Mel were here, he might have a chance of surviving the next two months.

God, he wished Mel was here.

Joe grabbed his drumsticks from his back pocket. Warming up, he twirled the sticks to a beat in his head as he followed the guys to the stage.

In front of a Marshall amp wall stood a woman in shredded jeans and a black tank top strumming a guitar. By her long black and blue hair, Joe recognized her. This wasn't good.

"Ivy fucking Page!" Dylan exclaimed. "No way!" He leaped up the stairs to the stage.

She stopped playing. "Fucking Gracefall." She put her hands on her hips. "How did I get so lucky?" Sarcasm dripped from every word. Dylan crashed into her, pulling her into a hug.

"Watch it!" She stepped back and pointed to her guitar. "Break it, and I kick your ass."

Joe and Tyler finally caught up. Ivy was Blushing Alice's lead guitarist—Dylan's ex-girlfriend's bandmate. He'd seen the band in action, and Ivy was one hell of a musician. She hit the power cord unlike any other. However, this was way too close for comfort. This was the exact thing he'd been worried about. Could he trust Dylan not to fall apart being this close to his ex's bandmate?

"You're our new guitarist?" Joe gave more attitude than he'd intended.

Tyler elbowed him and shot him a *be cool* look.

He ignored him and stood with his arms folded across his chest.

"I guess we can skip the introductions." She sauntered over to him in her knee-high, black suede stiletto boots. Gene Simmons in his platform boots had nothing on her. "I'm sorry to hear about Moxley. He's a legend." She turned her attention on Joe. "Listen, I'm here to save your asses. I have my own band. You guys have me for two months, then I'm back to Cali with Blushing Alice."

Inside, Joe sighed in relief. Regardless of Dylan and Ash's past, Gracefall had never had a woman in the group. This changed everything. He'd seen how the guys acted around Mel, and she was off limits. For fuck's sake, why did it have to be Ivy Page?

"Hey, I can tell you guys don't like this idea. I get it—Ash and Dylan drama. But in all honesty, I'm honored to have this opportunity to play with Gracefall. I won't mess it up. If this isn't good enough, then take it up with Davidson. He's the one who set this up."

Of course, he did. Both bands shared the same management and record label. But Joe couldn't help thinking this deal was a jab to Dylan. "No, we're cool. It's been a rough couple of weeks."

"Yep, no rest for the wicked." She gazed at her guitar and started strumming without the amp.

"Are you familiar with the song lineup?" Dylan asked. "We have some time to practice before the show."

Ivy sauntered back to the wall of Marshalls and plugged in. She turned to the guys, giving them their own private concert. The first cords of "Visiting Darkness" came wailing out of her guitar effortlessly. She shredded the strings, dropping it low, making it heavy. She played it perfectly with her own individual style. Mox would approve.

"Fuck yeah, dude!" Excited, Dylan grabbed his mic.

"She's a quick study." Tyler joined in, banging his head to the groove as he took his bass from its stand. A huge smile spread across Joe's face. This was exactly the ass-kicking they needed.

"Joseph, you want to drop us a beat?" Dylan sang in the deep growl he was famous for.

Hell yeah, he did. Joe jogged back to his kit and sat on his throne. He twirled his sticks, counting in the beat. With the first strike on the skins, he was in the zone—his zone.

24

*B*efore entering the concert hall, Melody tried calling Joe one more time. As the voicemail message played, she ended the call. It struck her as odd that he hadn't returned her calls all day, nor had he texted her explaining why he couldn't talk. As she chewed nervously on her thumbnail, she couldn't think of one reason for his silence. The summer tour had ended two days ago. Joe should be home, or at least on his way.

Up until now, she'd talked to him every night. They'd even had amazing phone sex a few times, which she'd never believed could be possible. But it wasn't the same. She missed his big arms wrapped around her, giving her the promise of forever. She missed the hot rush when they kissed.

However, their last conversation left her feeling uneasy about their relationship. There was a distance, as though something was distracting him. She knew losing Mox had been hard on everyone, especially Joe. But that was only part of it. Two months was a long time to be away from each other.

Insecurity wasn't something she was proud of, but it crept in, embedding doubt. It wasn't another woman she worried about. It was two friends falling out of love.

She checked the time. One hour before the show.

"Hey, Melody."

She looked up. Megan, a violinist in the orchestra, walked toward her. "Are you ready? The pre-concert lecture is starting."

Shaking free from the distraction, she turned off her cell. "Yeah." She smiled and followed Megan into the concert hall.

On stage, a row of five musicians dressed in black evening attire sat on barstools facing an audience of fifty fans, who were waiting to get up close and personal with the artists and composer. She loved this part of the night, when she talked about her passion and inspired people to play music. She was living proof hard work paid off—her dreams had come true.

In two months, her life had changed. After the trial audition, she'd landed her dream job. She had hours of practice under her belt. She'd played four concerts at four different local venues. She even had a small group of fans who came out only to see her. Yeah, she was living her dream. The one thing missing was Joe.

Before she knew it, she was walking on stage with her cello to her seat. She sat behind her cello and looked out into a full house. A smile spread across her face. It was no wonder they had pulled in a full house. The conductor was artistically adventurous and pushed the boundaries of the concert experience. The music was beautiful and edgy, and she loved playing it.

The lights dimmed, and the warm-up halted. Butterflies fluttered in her stomach as the conductor took his place behind a raised podium in front of the orchestra. He could easily be mistaken for an eighties rock star with his long black hair and a leather jacket. The audience went wild.

~

*T*he orchestra began, and Joe took his seat in the back of the concert hall, keeping a low profile. He wanted all attention on Mel. One look at her, and his heart ached. He hated lying to her. It made him feel sick. He'd been back home for two days and staying in a hotel. He wanted to surprise her, since he hadn't been able to attend one of her concerts. He hoped she wouldn't be too mad.

She was beautiful on stage, playing her cello with unmatched grace and talent. Her long blonde hair was pulled up high on her head. What he wouldn't do to kiss her neck right now. It drove him mad not being able to touch her. He'd missed her like crazy. The black dress she wore showed off her long, tan legs. She was the sexiest cellist he'd ever seen, and he was sure the guys in the front few rows thought the same thing.

Joe was proud of the young woman she'd become. She'd worked hard, and now her dreams were coming true. It was about time. She sounded amazing.

He shifted in his seat, uncomfortable in the suit he wore. Looking at the audience, he could have gotten away with wearing his jeans and concert tee.

Wasn't life crazy? His childhood best friend was his lover. He still pinched himself every day—Melody Sterling, rock and roll royalty, was in love with him, the kid from the trailer park.

They both had dared to dream, and it had paid off.

The orchestra mesmerized him and got him thinking.

The rock tone of the pieces was amazing. What would it take to get the LA Orchestra to play on the next Gracefall album? He thumbed through the concert pamphlet, looked through the directory, and made a note of the conductor. He was serious. He needed to meet this guy.

They still hadn't found a guitarist. There had been rumors about management holding an audition in a few weeks, but nothing had been finalized. At this point, he couldn't think about it. Melody was on his mind. And if all the stars lined up, he'd be in her bed tonight, making up for lost time.

The orchestra took a bow, ending the show. The audience gradually filed out of the hall. Joe stayed behind, waiting for the crowd to thin out. Once it was clear, he made his way outside, where some of the orchestra musicians were hanging out with fans. Across the courtyard, he saw Melody holding a glass of champagne and talking to a group of women.

Joe walked toward her; their eyes met. Her smile faded as he got closer. Well, this wasn't what he'd expected. The women left, and Mel stood frozen.

"Hey, you," he said as he closed the distance between them. "You sounded amazing tonight."

"What are you doing here?" He was taken aback by her bleak tone. Had something changed between them? Were they back in friends-only territory? If they were, he hadn't picked up on it until now.

"I mean." She shook her head. "Oh my god, you're here!" She set her glass down on a nearby table and threw her arms around his neck. Hell yeah, that's what he was expecting.

Joe squeezed her tight. "I wanted to surprise you." He handed her a bouquet of a dozen roses.

"These are gorgeous." She quickly examined the flowers, then turned her attention back on him. "You cut your hair, and you wore a suit."

He rubbed the newly shaven mohawk. "Yeah, I thought these orchestra gigs were more refined."

She laughed. "Most are, but you're in LA, baby." She smiled brightly. "You look good."

They stood in silence as they took each other in. He hadn't realized how much he'd missed her until that moment.

"Why didn't you call me back?"

"I'm sorry. I didn't want to ruin my surprise. I've been here for two days. It's been hell not telling you."

"Well." She raised a brow. "I guess I can't be mad. I'm flattered you came to see me tonight. I've missed you, Rock Star."

God, he loved the flirty tone in her voice. "I've missed you, too." He dipped down and claimed her lips, sliding his tongue into her mouth to dance with hers. It felt good having her in his arms again.

She broke the kiss and caught her breath. "How long do we have before you leave?"

Resting his forehead against hers, he played with fallen tendrils of hair around her neck. "Long enough to find a guitarist and get back on the road. Davidson wants us back on tour so we don't lose momentum."

"We shouldn't waste any time." She held her bottom lip between her teeth, playfully gazing up at him. And didn't that send a message straight to his dick?

He gave her a wicked smile. "I agree." He took her hand and pulled her toward the parking lot.

"Where are we going?" She giggled as she tried to keep up.

"I have a limo waiting."

"Wait, I have my car here. I can't leave it."

"You're not."

They reached the black stretch sedan. He walked over to the driver, who'd been waiting to open his door, and gave him fifty bucks. "Give me an hour."

The driver took the money and smiled, then went on an hour stroll.

Joe turned to her and smiled wickedly. "Ever have sex in a limo?" He knew the answer was no, but he still teased.

"No." She blushed. He loved seeing her cheeks flush. "Have you?"

"Nope. Saving that experience for you." He opened the car door. "After you."

"Are you serious?"

"As a heart attack." He pulled her close. "We have more room in the limo than your sports car."

She shook her head. "You're something else."

"But you love me," he winked.

"I do. I love you, Joe Grace."

"I love you, Mel." He brushed her cheek with the back of his knuckles and stared into her hazel eyes. "From the first time I set eyes on you, I loved you."

He'd spend the rest of his life loving her, or for as long as she'd have him.

25

*M*elody pulled into her driveway after a full day of practice. The sun would be setting soon. She couldn't wait to have a glass of wine on her back balcony and share the beautiful sunset with the man she loved. Life couldn't get any better.

Even though she was tired and her hands ached from playing an intense piece of a new song she was learning for the next concert, the thought of coming home to Joe renewed her. She smiled as she put the car in park. She couldn't believe it. She was playing cello on a song her boyfriend had written. The music director at the orchestra had agreed to add a Gracefall song to their lineup. Joe had really hit it off with the conductor, who had helped compose an instrumental version of Gracefall's hit, "Surrender to the Unknown."

Life was good.

She'd had Joe all to herself for two whole weeks. Well, mostly to herself. He had band business to settle and an audition for a new guitarist coming up, which to her surprise, he was handling well. He'd be leaving to go on tour again soon, but she wasn't wasting precious time thinking about it. Every free minute she had, she wanted to be with Joe.

Melody got out of the car and hurried inside. "Hey, I'm home," she called out as she kicked her shoes off.

Joe didn't answer.

Where was he?

As she walked toward the kitchen, she saw a trail of red rose petals leading to the bedroom. Her body heated as she thought about what was in the bedroom waiting for her. She bit her bottom lip and smiled. What was Joe up to?

Melody followed the flowers to her room. She looked around. No Joe on her bed.

She continued following the trail, which led her to the bathroom. The garden tub was sprinkled in red petals and candles. A glass of wine sat on the edge, waiting for her.

She didn't know what Joe was up to, but she'd play along.

Melody twisted her hair up into a bun, then undressed. She stepped into the tub. The temperature was perfect. She leaned back and submerged herself into the soothing water. It was heaven.

She took the wine glass and sipped leisurely as she looked out the window at a breathtaking view. The wall of windows overlooked the mountains in her backyard. Swatches of bright red, yellow, and orange filled the sky as the sun set.

Music began playing softly. Joe walked in with a towel wrapped around his waist. "Hey, beautiful." He bent down and kissed her. "Mind if I join you?"

"I think there's room for two," she teased.

His towel dropped. So did her gaze. She'd never seen a more handsome, perfectly built man.

He slid in behind her. His big body filled the tub, but she didn't care. Strong arms pulled her close as she lay back against him. They sat in silence and watched the sun disappear behind the mountain peak. In his arms, the world melted away. These were the memories she'd bottle up and keep forever.

Taking in his warmth, she sighed.

"You like your surprise?" he asked, whispering.

The coarseness of his beard brushing against her neck sent a shiver through her. "I do. A girl could get used to this. What's the occasion?"

"I just wanted to see you naked."

She laughed. "You are so bad." She splashed him.

"Nah, just a boy in love."

"Well, if this is bad, then you can be bad every day."

"Every day?"

"Yep."

"Does this mean like being bad forever?"

"As long as it's with me."

"That's a deal."

A small cream-colored box appeared in front of her. What was he doing? He opened the box. "Melody Sterling, will you marry me?"

Melody's eyes widened, taking in the impressive diamond. Her heart pounded, and her hand shook as he placed the engagement ring on her finger. Was she dreaming?

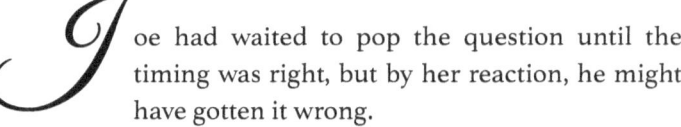

*J*oe had waited to pop the question until the timing was right, but by her reaction, he might have gotten it wrong.

He wanted the night to be perfect, something she wouldn't forget. He didn't have the time to whisk her away to an exotic place and pop the question. However, he wasn't leaving without asking. She needed to know he was serious about their relationship. She was his one and only.

The silence was killing him. Didn't she want to get married? Of course, she did, or at least he'd thought so. He rubbed the tension from the back of his neck. It had to be the ring. He'd screwed up on the ring. "Baby, if you don't like it, I can exchange it."

She turned and faced him. "The ring is perfect."

Thank God. Relief washed over him. Then what was the problem?

"Joe, this is crazy." She shook her head.

He didn't need to be a genius to know what was running through her mind. She was afraid they would end up like her parents. "Mel, we're nothing like your parents. There will never be another woman in my life but you. Besides, you have to say yes."

Her face turned to suspicion. "I do?"

"Yes, I went through a lot of trouble to get your parents' blessings. We have your dad's blessing."

She rolled her eyes. "Of course. He loves you."

"And your mother's."

"You're joking, right?"

"No jokes. I had brunch with her this morning. Lovely woman." He tried not to sound sarcastic, but the woman scared the hell out of him.

"Was she on her best behavior?"

"I left there with my balls still intact, so yeah."

She shook her head. "I can't believe you actually got her blessing."

He held her face in his hands tenderly. "Your parents

want you to be happy. I want to make you happy. You're my one and only, Mel. So, what do you say?"

She nodded. Tears filled her eyes. "Yes, I will marry you, Joe Grace." She lunged forward and threw her arms around his neck.

He held her tight. The warm fuzzies filled his heart. His childhood best friend had said yes to being his wife. Lucky bastard.

"I love you," he said softly.

She rested her forehead against his. Her hands caressed the Celtic cross tattoo on his chest, tracing her name with her fingertips. "I love you, Rock Star."

Sometime between Melody joining him on tour and now, the meaning of his tattoo had changed. Their friendship was no longer his cross to bear. She'd saved him. He held her hand over the tattoo. "You're my saving grace, Mel."

She gazed deeply into his eyes. "Joe."

"It's true. I don't know where I'd be if it wasn't for you." He claimed her mouth, kissing her softly. "I think we need to seal the deal on this engagement."

A big smiled formed across her lips. "Most definitely." She straddled him.

He didn't know what the future held for Gracefall, but with Mel by his side, he could get through anything. He'd spend the rest of his days making her happy. He could have it all—the band and his woman.

EPILOGUE

*J*oe and Melody walked into The Black Veil nightclub where Davidson and Kimmy had set up for the audition. It had been a sweet deal for Joe. He didn't have to take part in all the pre-audition bull-shit. Through Davidson's connections, they'd already had a good list of candidates. All he had to do was show up and play. The hard part was deciding who would replace Mox.

"Hi, Joe," Davidson greeted. He nodded to Melody. "There's a list of auditionees on the table. First audition starts in thirty."

"Do the auditionees know the songs we'll be playing?"

"Nope, baptism by fire, baby. If they want a shot, they better have done their homework."

"Yep." Feeling numb and a sense of betrayal to Mox, Joe went over the compiled list of auditionees that corporate had pre-screened. Out of the five guitarists, he'd only heard of one of the artists, a successful, well-known hired gun who'd played with a few big-name bands, Elliot Phoenix. Now, that was impressive. There was an asterisk by her name explaining that the audition would be held the next night.

Joe exhaled, calming his nerves. This didn't feel right. Mox should be here.

"Hey." He felt Melody caress his shoulder. "You can do this, babe."

"I don't know." He rubbed the stress from the back of his neck. "This doesn't feel right."

"I know, but it has to be done." She looked at him, and he instantly felt comforted. "I'll be right over there," she pointed at the bar, "making my pros and cons list for every auditionee."

He smiled. That was his Melody—always having his back. He cupped her face and kissed her. "I love you."

"I love you, Rock Star." She gave him a grin, then left toward the bar, letting him get to work.

He walked toward the stage where Dylan and Tyler were looking through the song list.

"These fuckers better be musically sound to tackle these songs." Dylan handed the list to Joe. "Corporate ain't fucking around."

He looked over the songs. "Shit, no one will come close to executing Mox's solo on "Releasing Anger." He shook his head. His mind was already made up. Every single artist coming in today wasn't good enough. Mox was irreplaceable. It would take an act of God to fill his friend's boots.

"Let's keep an open mind," Tyler reminded him. "Personality over virtuosity." He grabbed his bass and thumbed a few notes.

"Yeah, but they have to hold their own musically," Dylan added. "I'm not a fucking teacher."

Joe made his way on stage, spinning his sticks. "Don't worry. Melody is making a pros and cons list for every candidate. She'll have a guitarist nailed down by the end of the day."

The guys laughed, then quickly sobered as Joe called them over. "Group meeting."

They huddled together.

"I know this isn't going to be easy. No one's replacing Moxley. We're doing this for the future of Gracefall."

"Fuck yeah, dude." Joe felt Dylan's excitement.

"Mox would want this," Tyler added. "We need to find the right guy—"

"Or chick," Dylan added with a sly grin.

"With the right chemistry and goals like ours."

"Agreed," Dylan concurred.

Joe hesitated, Dylan and Tyler's eyes on him. As much as he wanted to believe his own pep talk, it still felt wrong. This wound was deep, and there was no bandage big enough to stop the bleeding.

He glanced up at Melody and was rewarded with an encouraging smile. Yep, he had this. He looked at Tyler then Dylan. This was his family. Together, they'd get through this. "One-hundred percent agreed."

They broke the huddle, and the guys took their places. The front door opened, and all eyes followed. A dude looking like he'd just stepped out of an eighties glam band walked in with his six-string strapped to his back and a black leather jacket with fringe hanging from the arms. He met with Davidson, signed in, then strutted to the stage.

Dylan looked back at Joe with a "what the fuck dude" look. Joe shook his head, then looked at Tyler, who was holding in a laugh.

Dylan turned his attention back on the auditionee. "Fuck no!" he pointed to the door the guy just walked in from.

"What?" The guy stood stunned. "I haven't played yet."

Dylan didn't respond. He turned his back and walked toward Joe's drum kit.

"What the fuck!" Frustrated, Joe dropped his sticks. "This is what we get for allowing corporate to choose auditionees."

"Dude doesn't fit our brand," Tyler huffed.

Dylan looked over his shoulder, inspecting the guy's outfit. "Hell, I wouldn't be caught wearing that jacket, and I like fringe."

As the guys conversed, the guitar solo of "Surrender to the Unknown" belted out behind them. All the cords were played perfectly yet sounded nothing like Mox. Joe's mouth dropped open as he motioned to the guys to turn around.

The jacket had been tossed, and the dude was shredding his Gibson Les Paul like a guitar god. "Who the fuck is this guy?" Dylan asked Joe.

"I have no idea," he replied, stunned.

The three of them looked in awe as the guy transitioned into "Releasing Anger."

Joe dropped a beat, and Tyler followed his lead on bass. Dylan motioned for the guy to come on stage as he sang the chorus. Joe couldn't believe his ears. Leather jacket dude was killing it. There had to be a rub somewhere. One audition and they'd found their guy—no way!

The song ended, and the four of them stood staring at each other. Joe didn't want to admit it, but the jam had felt good, damn good.

"Who the fuck are you, dude?" Dylan asked as he shook the guy's hand.

"Jake Quinn. I'm a studio musician. You can find all my work on my YouTube channel."

"Like a hired gun?" Tyler asked.

"Mostly studio work."

Joe joined the guys in front of his drum kit. "Do you have any experience being in a band?"

"I've played in a few. Mostly local and at the bar I own, Quincy's."

"I've heard of Quincy's," Tyler chimed in. "Isn't that in Reno?"

"Yep."

"So, what are your feelings about touring? We're on the road most of the year. Are willing to travel?" Joe asked.

"Absolutely. One-hundred percent committed."

"What about your bar?"

"No worries there," Jake reassured. "Listen, my dream is to play in a band and to make good music. The outfit was just to get your attention so I would stand out from the rest. I know, poorly executed."

"Dude, you totally achieved cringe-worthiness," Dylan laughed.

Joe was still stunned. They had found a dude who rocked their balls off, and they got along? Never happens. "So, listen Jake. I think you've awed us today, but we still have three auditionees coming in and one tomorrow night."

"Right." Jake removed his guitar. "Understandable."

"Things look good, really good. We'll be in touch soon." Joe shook his hand.

"Thank you for the opportunity."

"Words of advice." Dylan shook Jake's hand. "Burn the jacket, dude."

About Victoria Zak

Victoria Zak is an internationally bestselling author of historical and contemporary romance. She weaves magic into her timeless tales, reminding readers anything is possible, especially with a dragon by your side. Raised in Dunedin, Florida, the sister city to Stirling, Scotland, no wonder she grew up fascinated with anything Scottish. Add the ocean into the mix, and it's easy to see where Victoria found inspiration for her stories.

As a child, she read anything she could get her hands on, which developed into full-scale book addiction by adulthood. Curious by nature, Victoria doesn't shy away from anything. She enjoys historical research and hanging out at the nearest coffee shop. Victoria currently resides in Maryland with her real-life heroes, her husband and two children.

Victoria loves to hear from her readers. You can connect with her through the links below:

www.victoriazakromance.com
victoria@victoriazakromance.com
Newsletter http://bit.ly/1uebjmR

facebook.com/VictoriaZakAuthor

bookbub.com/authors/victoria-zak

instagram.com/victoriazakromance

twitter.com/VictoriaZak2

BOOKS BY VICTORIA ZAK

Graceful: Vicious Love Tour Series

Rock Me to the Top

Rock the Line (2021)

Rocked and Bothered (2021)

Been Caught Rockin' (2022)

Guardians of Scotland Series:

Highland Burn

Highland Storm

Highland Fate

Highland Destiny

Highland Hope

Highland Unleashed (2022)

Ember Brooke Series:

Scorched Hearts

Hearts Under Fire

Daughters of Highland Darkness Series:

Beautiful Darkness

Deadly Darkness

Wicked Darkness

Stand Alones:

Once Upon a Winter Solstice

The Jewel of Grim Fortress

Midnight's Kiss

www.ingramcontent.com/pod-product-compliance
Lightning Source LLC
Chambersburg PA
CBHW020603180626
46810CB00007B/2631